PIONEER YEARNING

THE O'ROURKE FAMILY MONTANA SAGA, BOOK THREE

RAMONA FLIGHTNER

GRIZZLY DAMSEL PUBSLISHING

For You, Dear Reader:
Thank you for your
passion for my writing
and for embracing
this new series.

CHAPTER 1

Fort Benton, Montana Territory; October 1865

The pouring rain prevented many of the townsfolk from attending the funeral. Anyone related to the deceased man, dedicated to those mourning or foolish enough to otherwise attend stood next to the gaping hole, dripping from the incessant fall deluge. The priest's voice, nearly drowned out by the sound of the downpour pelting hats and the ground, rose as he said his final prayer.

Those gathered looked to the widow, eager for her to get on with it, so they could return to their homes or the saloons.

"Does she want the priest to have more business?" one man muttered, as he stared at the woman standing stock-still as she peered into the yawning hole in front of her.

"Still can't believe Dunmore found a priest so near winter," another murmured.

"No one can deny an O'Rourke," a third grumbled.

Unaware of the murmuring and the speculation around her, Niamh O'Rourke Ahern stared into her husband's grave. She bent, scooping up a handful of mud to sprinkle over his casket. Rather than the priest's final blessing ringing in her ears, she heard the final words her husband had spoken to her, before he had stormed out of their house that fateful night.

Her hand shook as she opened her palm, the mud landing on the casket in a *splat*. Thankful for the rain, it concealed the fact she did not cry for Connor. How could she mourn such a man?

At her father's urging, she turned away from the grave to return to her family home and to her daughter, Maura, ignoring the echo of her husband's words, as though carried on the vicious wind.

I never loved you, you faithless harpy.

～

Cormac Ahern stood beside his brother's grave, long after all the other mourners had departed. Against his will, he had watched Niamh leave, leaning against her father for support, as her brothers hovered around her. He fought anger and rage at all that had transpired.

"Damn you, Connor," he rasped, as he swiped at his face, smearing tears, snot, dirt, and raindrops across his bearded cheeks. "How could you do this to her?" He closed his eyes, as he knew he would have one-sided conversations with his brother for the rest of his life. How was it that his beloved elder brother was dead?

Swaying, he fell to his knees and bowed his head, taking off his hat in deference to his deceased brother. "I shouldn't swear at you. Not on the day of your burial." He slammed his hand onto the packed-down earth. "But how could you?" he asked again, his shoulders shaking with sobs. "We were supposed to go through life together. Fight all our battles together."

He put his hat back on, ignoring the horrible weather. Today he refused to remember the distance that had sprouted up between him and his brother since they had arrived in Fort Benton. The disappointment and the frustration which Cormac had felt in equal measure. Instead he mourned what should have been. What *could* have been.

A hand squeezed his shoulder, and he looked up into the eyes of Ardan O'Rourke, the eldest son of Seamus O'Rourke. "Come, Cormac. You'll give yourself pneumonia, sittin' out here in the rain, an' you know Connor would never want that for you." He took a step back, granting Cormac a few more moments alone beside his older brother's grave.

Finally Cormac stood and faced Ardan. "I can't go to your family's home tonight."

Ardan stood in front of him, as tall as Cormac, although not nearly as brawny. Cormac had earned his strong lean muscles from the hours steering a team of oxen hitched to supply wagons to various destinations throughout the Montana Territory. Ardan knew he could never force Cormac into doing something he didn't want to do. However, Cormac was as loyal to the family as any O'Rourke. "Niamh needs her family around her, Cormac. *All* of her family."

Swearing under his breath, Cormac ducked his head and kicked at a rock, inadvertently pushing it into a puddle. "Fine. I'll come for a few minutes. But then I'm leaving."

Ardan slapped him on his back, letting it rest there to give further solace to Cormac. "You won't want to leave. Not after you taste the fine whiskey Da unearthed."

"I thought we drank all the whiskey last night."

Ardan rubbed at his head with his free hand and shook his head with chagrin. "So did I, Cormac. So did I." He gave a slight tug on Cormac's shoulder, urging him into motion and away from the grave. Murmuring in a soft voice, he said, "You know we'll help with a gravestone. We'll ensure he's remembered."

Cormac jerked his head in acknowledgment, walking beside Ardan in silence to the large O'Rourke house. Although the two eldest O'Rourke sons, Ardan and Kevin, had married and no longer lived there, and the next three sons—Declan, Eamon, and Finn—were in Saint Louis for the winter, procuring supplies for their business, still the house was always full. Rarely did Ardan, Kevin, and their brides miss a family dinner together. And, since Connor's death, Niamh had moved home too, with her fifteen-month-old daughter, Maura.

Cormac paused at the back entrance of the kitchen, attempting to scrape the mud and the muck off his boots before entering. Crossing the threshold of the kitchen, he saw a makeshift clothes rack near the stove. He shucked his hat and jacket, adding them to the pile of clothes steaming by the range. With a shy smile, he accepted a towel from Mary O'Rourke, the matriarch of the large family. Of middling height, she had a presence about her that commanded the respect of all her family, although a distance remained between her and her daughter, Niamh. Unlike most of her children, Mary had auburn hair, now shot with gray, and her hazel eyes were always filled with compassionate concern.

"Wipe yourself down, lad," she said, as she fussed over him with a worried smile. "Seamus has set out dry clothes for you, if you like." Although she had never taken to Niamh's husband, she had shown an instant affinity for Cormac.

Flushing, Cormac shook his head. "There's no need," he protested, as he ran the towel over his long brown hair. "I shouldn't stay long."

Mary tugged at his arm, urging him into the living room. "You'll stay as long as you like. An', if you want to spend the night, there's room. With too many of my boys away, there's always a bed for you." She squeezed his arm. "Don't allow your grief to turn you into a hermit." She stood on her toes to kiss his cheek and returned to the kitchen and a large pot of soup she was preparing with her youngest daughter, Maggie.

Cormac paused at the entrance of the living room to find the O'Rourke men, standing and chatting in low voices, while the women sat near Niamh in a far corner. Although Niamh's hair was damp, she appeared to have changed into dry clothes, although they were no longer black. The indigo-blue dress enhanced her natural beauty, making her auburn hair shine. He frowned as it also highlighted the circles under her eyes and the desolation in her expression. Kevin's and Ardan's wives, Aileen and Deirdre, sat on either side of the widow.

Cormac forced himself to stop staring at Niamh and to approach the O'Rourke men. He absently noted the priest, warming himself near the potbellied stove, talking with Dunmore, a successful stagecoach driver and friend of the O'Rourkes. Cormac accepted a glass of whiskey from Kevin, the second-eldest brother and husband to Aileen. Ardan stood beside Seamus, their father. Younger brothers, Niall and Lucien, stood tall, as though honored to be included in the group of older men. However, the three youngest boys loitered nearby, although they had begun to fidget. Cormac understood their restlessness. If possible, he'd be outside wandering, rather than cooped up inside, spouting niceties.

Seamus clapped Cormac's arm, and he focused on the men around him. "'Tis a tragedy," Seamus murmured.

Cormac nodded and lowered his head. "Yes. But Connor had lived a wild life for too long. It was only a matter of time ..." He broke off what more he would have said and took a sip of his whiskey.

"We've all had wild times in our lives," Seamus murmured. "'Tis a shock what occurred." Seamus shared a quick look with his two eldest sons, who nodded subtly.

"Thank you for finding a priest," Cormac murmured. "I don't know how you managed that this time of year."

Seamus looked with gratitude in the direction of the stagecoach driver. "Dunmore has his ways," Seamus said. "An' I'm glad of it, for we wanted to honor Connor too. It wouldn't have been right, burying him without a proper prayer."

Cormac made a sound of agreement, taking another sip of whiskey, as his throat had thickened and he was incapable of speaking. The image of the yawning hole with his brother's casket inside filled his vision.

"I know you must believe that no one understands how you feel," Ardan murmured, recalling Cormac to the present, "but we have an idea of what today is like." He paused. "We remember what it was like to lose our mum."

Cormac nodded to acknowledge their sympathy. He knew well the story of Mary O'Rourke's separation from her family, upon their arrival from Ireland in 1847 in Montreal, Canada. She, and Seamus's youngest daughter, Maggie, had spent nearly eighteen years apart from them. Only in June of this year had they been reunited. However, Cormac fought a deep resentment because they had always had one another. They had never truly been alone, as Cormac now was. He paused as he took a deep breath to calm his anger and his grief. *Except for Mary*, he realized. She had been left alone with a newborn to care for. "Thank you," he finally rasped out, his voice roughened by his deep emotions.

Seamus cleared his throat and squeezed his shoulder, as though knowing instinctively what he thought. "You aren't alone, Cormac. You have all of us. We will always be your family."

A rising surge of emotions threatened to overwhelm him, and he thrust his whiskey glass at one of the youngest O'Rourke boys before fleeing the room. In the kitchen he snatched his hat and coat and raced outside into the rain. After a few steps, he shrugged into his jacket, jammed on his hat, and stormed away to his nearby one-room cabin. Grief and guilt threatened to swallow him whole. For, no matter what the O'Rourkes said, Cormac knew they would never be his family. How could they want him after what he did?

Niamh sat in a dazed stupor on the sofa, tears coursing down her cheeks. She gave silent thanks for the outward sign of bereavement, for now that she cried, there would be little gossip about the widow who failed to grieve for her feckless husband. Closing her eyes, she attempted to corral an inappropriate giddiness that she was free of Connor. Immediately after that thought, guilt at her lack of grief filled her. What kind of woman was she to feel relief at her husband's death?

When one of her sisters-in-law touched her arm, she jerked.

"Niamh," murmured Deirdre, Ardan's wife. "You will come through this. I promise. I know it seems unfathomable right now. But you will."

She nodded dumbly, for she didn't know what else to do.

Aileen spoke up, stroking her other arm. "You won't be alone. Your family will always be here to support you."

"I know," Niamh murmured. "It's hard to realize he was alive three days ago and now ..." Her voice faded away, as she swayed in place in her seat, her gaze distant and unfocused. "Now Maura doesn't have a father."

"No," Deirdre said in a soothing voice, "but she has plenty of uncles and a wonderful grandfather. She will never lack a man's love and support."

Niamh nodded over and over again. As though against her will, her gaze rose and met the mournful, rage-filled gaze of her brother-in-law, Cormac. More guilt and other emotions she had no desire to examine today swelled up in her, and she closed her eyes, unwilling to look into his beautiful blue eyes. Rather than the cobalt of her father's eyes, they were robin's-egg blue. Or sky blue. Depending on his feelings. She sighed, resenting how much time she had spent contemplating his eyes and the emotions hidden within. When she opened her eyes, Cormac had disappeared from the room.

"I wish I could dull how I feel with whiskey, as men do," she murmured. "Why are such escapes denied to women?"

Aileen and Deirdre shared worried smiles, as they scooted closer to Niamh. "It's the way of the world, love," Deirdre said. "Besides, I highly doubt you'd want to drink such a horrible beverage."

Niamh shrugged. Only at the sight of her daughter, Maura, did she brighten. "Oh, there's my little angel," she whispered. She held out her arms for her daughter and sighed with pleasure to hold her daughter in her arms. Maura snuggled into her mother's embrace and soon fell asleep. Ignoring the room filled with those paying their respects, or merely present to sip at her father's fine whiskey, Niamh rocked her daughter in place and tried to envision a day free of guilt, grief, and fear.

S eamus watched Niamh with concern, as she held her daughter. "I fear we didn't soothe the lad as we had hoped," he murmured to Ardan and Kevin, after Cormac had stormed away. "For some reason, he wants to keep himself apart from us."

Ardan shared a look with Kevin and then said in a soft voice, "He just lost his brother, Da. If I lost Kevin, or one of the other lads, I wouldn't be much for company." He cleared his throat, as though fighting a strong emotion at the thought of such a loss.

Kevin made a sound of agreement, and Seamus nodded.

"Aye. Makes me anxious to contemplate how Declan, Eamon, and Finn are coping during their stay in Saint Louis. I hate we'll have no news until they return home next summer." Seamus took a sip of whiskey, his cobalt-blue eyes filled with despair at the absence of three of his sons. "I want us all together again."

Kevin cleared his throat, as he looked at Niamh, who now held her daughter, Maura. "Did you notice she didn't cry at the grave?"

Seamus broke off what he was about to say when a man he did not know approached their small group.

"I'm sure I should offer condolences," said the man in an iridescent navy suit with matching waistcoat stretched over his small paunch. A mocking gleam in his eyes put a lie to his words.

"If one is drinking my whiskey, in my house, on the evening after the burial of my son-in-law, 'tis appropriate," Seamus said in a low voice.

"Ah, yes, the dearly departed. He'll be sorely missed, won't he?" the man asked, as he looked around the room at the clusters of townsfolk, speaking in low voices, before his gaze homed in on Niamh. "His widow, *Nee-am*, looks particularly devastated."

"You are not familiar with our ways, I see. My daughter's name is pronounced *Nee-ev*, akin to *leave* when drawn into two syllables," Seamus stated in his full Irish burr, standing taller, and nearer, to the irritating man. His brilliant blue eyes shone with dislike.

Ardan took a warning step toward the man. "Who are you, and what do you want?"

Puffing out his chest and smiling in an inappropriate manner in the wake-like atmosphere, he said, "Mr. Uriah Chaffee, Esquire, at your service."

"Well, Mr. Chaffee, we are thankful for your condolences. However, we are … engaged in mourning all that has been lost." Kevin placed a hand on his elder brother's arm, as he looked at Mr. Chaffee with an unveiled warning.

"Ah, yes, of course. Might I be permitted to call during your … involved mourning period? I must discuss a matter with you regarding the deceased's wishes." He smiled as though he had just declared "checkmate."

Seamus took a step toward him. "Your ways might be amusin' to those in a big city but not here, Mr. Chaffee. Here, we honor what we've lost." He waited, his eyes flashing with annoyance that Mr. Chaffee's smile failed to dim. "We'll see you in one week."

"Wonderful. One week it is. Please ensure the lovely widow is present. I'd hate for her to be deprived of hearing her late husband's last wishes." With eyes gleaming with anticipation, he melted into the crowd.

"Vile man," Lucien muttered.

"Aye," Niall agreed. "Will he cause trouble, Da?"

Seamus sighed, his gaze turned in the direction the lawyer had gone. "That sort of man always does, my boy." He took a sip of his whiskey. "Come. Let's not worry about what the weasel might say. We've worries enough today."

Cormac had every intention of ignoring the insistent knocking on his front door, but, when he heard the soft voice of Mary O'Rourke, he found himself rushing to open it. "Ma'am," he murmured in a near-reverent voice. "I—Why would you leave the gathering?" He stood tall, his suit coat slung over a nail in the corner, with his waistcoat half unbuttoned and his shirtsleeves rolled up. He flushed at his state of undress and began to do up his clothes.

"You know I don't care what you wear, Cormac," she said, with her gentle smile, as she tenderly cupped his face with one palm. "Might I come in? 'Tis a bit wet out tonight, although I should say it reminds me of Ireland."

He nearly smiled, something he had thought he would never do again, and stepped aside to allow her in. Belatedly he saw a small basket at her feet with a pot and a napkin inside. She picked it up and set the pot on the stove.

"You'll be wanting food at some point. Stew's in here, and there are a few pieces of brown bread wrapped up for you. 'Twill keep you full, until you're ready to venture out again."

"Why?" he whispered.

She ignored everything in the room but him—the shattered, devastated man who believed himself alone in the world. "Because you are part of my family, Cormac."

He shuddered at her words and shook his head, suddenly battling tears he refused to allow to fall. "No. I'm not. I don't deserve to be."

"Well, that's the beauty of it. I decide who's in my family, aye?" She ran a hand over his strong shoulders, whispering, "And I've claimed you as one of my own, *a mhac.*" When he shook his head at her Irish, she murmured, "My son."

His tears overflowed, and he whispered, "I don't deserve you, ma'am."

"*Mary,*" she said, as she pulled him into her arms. "An' you do. But you must believe you do as well." She stroked a hand over his strong back. "Just as you must believe you aren't alone. Your brother died a tragic death, but you are still with us. Unlike the time I was cruelly separated from my family and truly alone, you aren't, Cormac. You still have us. Never forget that."

She eased him away and looked deeply into his gaze. "My prayer for you is that you will live the life he never had the courage to. Filled with love and honor." She patted his cheek and slipped from his house.

Cormac collapsed into a chair, his mind whirling with the day's events. He yearned for the kinship Mary offered but feared she would retract her affection once she realized his sins.

Two days later, Niamh walked the short distance to Cormac's house. A cool breeze blew, although the sun peeked through the clouds, drying all but the deepest puddles after the recent deluge. She pulled her shawl around her at the hint of winter in the air. Taking a deep breath, she knocked on his door.

When it opened, he stood in shadows, his expression largely obscured. When he stepped into the light, she backed up a step at his forbidding expression.

"Niamh, stop," he said.

She froze, her gaze darting to his.

"You know I'll never hurt you."

She looked at him a long moment and then nodded. When he stepped aside and motioned for her to enter his cabin, she slipped inside. She glanced around the small one-room cabin, which she had never before entered. He had always visited her at the home she had shared with Connor. In the rear corner was a large bed, piled high with blankets and a few pillows. On the opposite wall was a table where two could sit, with a window casting light into the room. Another window, beside the front door, allowed more light into the small space. A potbellied stove sat on bricks and stood in the corner to the right, with two chairs in front of it. "Two of everything?" she asked.

Cormac flushed and rubbed at his nape. "It had always been Connor and me. I hoped he'd stop for a visit." His gaze dropped to the floor, and he looked away.

Niamh closed her eyes in regret, for she knew her husband, and she knew Connor would never have deigned to spend his time in conversation with his brother. Not when he could have been at the saloons, swigging firewater or gambling. "I'm sorry, Cormac."

He shrugged. "I should have expected no better. I'm the fool for ever thinking he'd be different than he was." He motioned her to a chair near the mostly dormant stove. "But fortunately it means I have seats for both of us when you visit." He poked at the embers in the stove and set kindling inside, waiting for it to catch before building up the fire.

Niamh sat in silence as she watched the fire, comfortable, the tension of the day seeping away. This is how she had always felt with Cormac. At ease. Secure. Her mind shied away from the word *safe*, but she knew, deep inside, that was truly how she felt. Silence between them never led to discord. Never came from discord. Instead it resulted from a deep understanding of the need for quiet communion and for the comfort brought by the mere presence of one who is cherished.

"I'm sorry," she blurted out, breaking the silence after over one-quarter hour. By this time, the fire had been built up, and the small cabin was quite warm.

"What for?" he asked, tossing the poker from one hand to the other.

"For causing his death," she whispered. She raised her tormented gaze to meet his penetrating one. "For exulting in it."

He sighed and dropped the poker to the floor, where it clattered against the metal shovel and broom for the stove, provoking a jarring *clang*. "If you did otherwise, you wouldn't be human. And I'd have you no other way than how you are." He pinched the bridge of his nose. "What will you do?"

She shook her head, staring into the flames. "I don't know, but I won't jump into the river." Her words evoked a soft smile from him, as she raised her gaze, and they shared a long look. They had teased each other about jumping in the river, since nearly the first day they had met on the steamboat.

Unbidden, a scene from two and a half years ago flitted through her mind.

A soft breeze blew as a pelican swooped by the side of the steamboat, as though discerning what sort of creature was invading the river. Niamh stood with her hair tied in a long braid down her back, marveling at the stark beauty of the barren land and the distant cliffs, as the steamboat made its slow progress up the river, battling its way through waters swollen with spring runoff. Frequently she heard crewmen calling a warning to the captain about floating logs and snags seen poking from the floor of the riverbed. Thankfully the captain had, so far, been adept enough to miss all such potential calamities.

"Have you had enough?" asked a man in his teasing, rich voice. "Contemplating jumping overboard?"

She giggled as Cormac nudged her in the shoulder with his. "Of course not. I'd never do such a thing." She lowered her voice to a barely audible level. "Not unless the ship were on fire, but then I fear I'd drown. I don't know how to swim."

He winked at her. "Never fear, Miss O'Rourke. I'd save you."

She shook her head but giggled again. "Always so gallant, Mr. Ahern."

"Cormac," he said with a smile. "When I hear Mr. Ahern, I think of my father." Then his smile turned to a grimace.

She shifted so she stood fully in the shade, with the breeze ruffling her hair, teasing tendrils of her auburn hair loose. She studied him for a long moment. He was tall, with brown hair that hung past his shoulders and sky-blue eyes. He was taller than his older brother, Connor, who had blond hair and muddy brown eyes. "Was your father a bad man?" she asked.

"No, of course not," Cormac said and then sighed. After a long moment, he murmured, "It makes me miss him. Them." When Niamh remained quiet, he said, "I grew up with a large family. In Missouri. My father was from Ireland. Left before the famine." He shrugged. "He never said why he left Ireland, but, after roaming for a while, he settled in Missouri, and he sweet-talked my mother into marrying him." His eyes gleamed for a moment, as though remembering long-distant scenes. "He always told the best stories. And spun everything to his advantage. He had a way of sweet-talking everyone."

"Like your brother," Niamh said with a sigh.

Cormac cleared his throat. "Yes, like Connor. And that isn't always a good thing, Miss O'Rourke. You must discern if any substance is behind the sweetness." He paused as he saw her think through his words, and her muti-

nous expression appeared, as she had no desire to give credence to his warn-ing. "Anyway, there were seven of us, with only one sister. And never enough food and always too much work on the farm. Connor and I were the eldest sons, and my da sent us away to sell our crops in a nearby market."

Niamh frowned. "Why didn't he go?"

Shrugging, Cormac rested his shoulder against a post. "He'd tried to swindle one of the merchants at the last market and thought Connor and I would be more accepted than he would be. And we were." His gaze clouded. "We were gone longer than planned, as the horse threw a shoe, and the axle on our cart broke. After five days away, we returned, to find everyone dead."

"What?" Niamh gasped. She gripped Cormac's arm. "How? What happened?"

"We don't know. Some sort of illness. But they all perished. And we didn't because we were at the market."

"Oh, Cormac, I'm so sorry," she whispered. "I thought it was awful to lose my mum and sister."

He squeezed her hand. "And it was, Miss O'Rourke. Never doubt it." He sighed as he looked over her shoulder. "Here comes, Connor, hoping to see you."

Niamh fought a squeal as she brushed at her hair. "Oh, I wish I looked more polished."

"You're beautiful, lass," he said. "Never doubt it."

Niamh barely heard him as she spun to see his charming older brother strolling in her direction, his golden hair glinting in the sun. Her sense of kinship to him had heightened to realize he had suffered loss too. She never registered Cormac leaving, her attention wholly focused on Connor.

"Niamh," Cormac repeated, breaking her reverie.

She started, her gaze focusing on the small cabin and then Cormac. She shivered, as though finally hearing his warning from years ago. She fought despair that she hadn't heeded it then. "Do you ever wonder, Cormac, what might have happened if things had been different?" She gazed at him with a desolate, confused gaze. "If I had chosen differently?" she whispered.

"Only every day," he muttered, rising to move to one of the

windows, his back now to her. "But I've found it does little to alter reality."

She rose, moving to his door. "I have a sense everything changed the day he died. I'm just waiting to see what is to come." With those words, she eased open his door to return to her parents' house, leaving him staring at her through his window.

CHAPTER 2

Three days after the funeral, Niamh walked behind her parents' house with her daughter. Maura was of an age where she loved to play outside, and Niamh knew that winter would come soon enough. Although she had no desire to do anything but lay in bed, she wanted to spend time with Maura, hoping her daughter could lift her out of her dark mood.

She stood in the dried, brittle grass, still damp after a frost, watching Maura frolic, as she chased small insects hatching in the warmer afternoon air in her halting little girl run where she always seemed on the verge of toppling over. However, Maura managed to keep her balance, and always pushed Niamh away when she wanted to run and play. Tilting her head up to the sun, Niamh sighed at the momentary pleasure of feeling the warmth on her cheeks. At the soft breeze blowing, rather than the harsh weather they had suffered in recent days, she clenched her hands together tightly, as she fought memories and attempted to live in the moment.

"Mrs. Ahern," a woman said, her soft voice interrupting Niamh's quiet interlude.

Niamh spun and gaped at the woman who had the temerity to speak with her. Although Aileen worked as a seamstress for Madam

Nora—the owner of Fort Benton's most successful brothel, called the Bordello—Niamh had never conversed with the woman. And, even though it had been rumored her father was friendly with the woman, Niamh had always discredited such gossip. "I'm uncertain why you would want to speak with me."

Madam Nora stood a few inches shorter than Niamh. Unlike Niamh's blatant beauty, Madam Nora appeared mouselike with brown hair, brown eyes, and nondescript features. However, her eyes shone with intelligence, and Niamh knew that the Madam was not one to be crossed or to be underestimated.

"I am here because I fear I am at your mercy." Rather than the skimpy, shiny clothes Niamh imagined a brothel owner would flaunt, Madam Nora wore a demure purple wool dress with a high neckline, and her polished black boots poked out from under the hem of her long skirts.

"I'm afraid I don't understand what you mean." Niamh glanced in the direction of her daughter and sighed with relief to see Maura building a fort out of sticks she had found.

"Your husband."

Niamh faced her, a tension thrumming through her at the mention of Connor.

"He died at my establishment," Nora said.

"Yes," Niamh said, "I had been informed of that … unfortunate occurrence." Niamh met Nora's gaze.

Nora watched her with a quizzical expression. "I'm uncertain you understand the full implications." Nora firmed her jaw and took a step closer to Niamh. She lowered her voice, as though wanting to prevent the possibility of her words carrying on the wind and reaching innocent Maura. "Your husband arrived at the Bordello, drunk and angry. Unfortunately Ezra was already dealing with an overly amorous customer."

Nora paused when Niamh snorted at the implication that such a customer in the Bordello were a rarity.

"Not all men treat women well when they are with them in private, but we do not allow them to mistreat the Sirens," Nora snapped. She flushed, and then her gaze sharpened as she saw Niamh shift with discomfort at her words. "As for your husband, he arrived during one of the rare moments when the front door was unattended by Ezra. Mr. Ahern took a shine to one of the Sirens and then attempted to abuse her."

Niamh sighed. "He always believed a little discomfort made the woman more amenable to his advances," she murmured.

Nora snorted her disagreement. "Well, my Siren was having none of it. She is highly sought after here, and she, nor any of my girls, need suffer a man's attention if they intend to harm her." She paused. "Your husband fought with Ezra, and he died."

Niamh stared at her a long moment. "Ah, you're worried about Ezra. Is he your man?"

"Yes, he's the man who works the front door. My security for the girls and a decent man."

Shaking her head, Niamh said, "No, *your* man."

Smiling, Nora shook her head. "No. Ezra and I share a purely collegial relationship. But he is like a brother to me."

Niamh turned away a moment, watching her daughter play with joyful abandon as she chased a butterfly, before tripping and falling. Rather than cry with frustration and run to her mother for a hug, she chortled with laughter and pushed herself up to continue her chase. Niamh blinked back tears, wondering where her own resilience, her own joy in life had gone. Why couldn't she be more like her daughter?

With a deep breath, she spoke in a soft voice. "I'd hate it if anything were to happen to one of my brothers. Or Cormac," she whispered. "I knew my husband well, Madam. I know what he was capable of." She faced Nora, her expression bleak, echoes of the mistreatment she had suffered in her gaze. "I won't press charges. Someway, somehow, I always suspected Connor would die a violent death. I see no point in ruining any more lives over the choices he made."

Madam Nora exhaled the breath she had been holding. She reached forward, squeezing Niamh's hand, as she blinked back tears. "Thank you."

Niamh nodded, focusing on her daughter again, as the sound of the Madam's footsteps fading away became more distant, until only the wind and her daughter could be heard. Niamh whispered to herself, "If he hadn't died by Ezra's hand, I fear he would have died by mine." At that thought, she shivered and forced herself to join her daughter, as Niamh attempted to forget the years she had spent with Connor Ahern.

~

A rdan sat in the kitchen of the café his wife ran, flirting with her, as few customers were here on this early October day. The townsfolk would arrive later for their supper, and they understood the café closed by seven thirty this time of year, so Ardan and Deirdre could join the O'Rourke family for their supper. He sighed when he heard the bell over the café door ring and winked at his wife before rising.

He entered the café seating area on quiet feet and stopped, watching as Cormac stood rocking in place, as though fighting an indecisiveness about whether he should stay or go. Ardan took a moment to study the man who had always held himself distant from the O'Rourkes, although they had considered him part of the family.

The loss of his brother had seemed to cause Cormac to lose that inherent sense of purpose that always filled him. Now it appeared as though he were floundering. The finality of Connor's loss had provoked a rootlessness evident to those who knew Cormac well.

Ardan approached him and held out his hand. "Cormac?" He watched him with a quizzical expression. "Why didn't you come in the back door? It's how the family always enters, and we eat together in the kitchen."

Cormac shook his head. "I ... I really shouldn't be considered family." He cleared his throat. "I came by to let you know I've decided I should leave Fort Benton."

Shaking his head, Ardan gripped his shoulders, anger and frustration shining in his cobalt-blue eyes. "No, Cormac. No." He paused to see if Cormac would speak and then said, "You are Maura's uncle. You are a part of our family. Don't leave when Niamh needs you."

Cormac jerked back, as though Ardan's words had provoked bodily harm. "The last thing Niamh needs is me." Guilt flashed in his gaze before he lowered his focus to the floor. "I thought you should know, so you could tell your family. I plan to leave in a few days. Spend the winter in Helena or Virginia City."

"But you'll come back? Fort Benton will be your base again?" Ardan asked.

Cormac shrugged, his expression filled with desolation. "I don't know. This was our dream. And now he's dead." He cleared his throat, as he held a hand over his eyes. "I can't envision remaining here."

Before he could stride away, Ardan asked in a quiet, piercing voice, "Do you believe Connor would have approved of you abandoning Niamh? Of leaving Maura, when she desperately needs a reminder of her father?"

Spinning to face Ardan, Cormac's expression was ablaze with stark misery as he strode to Ardan. "The last thing that little girl needs is a reminder of Connor."

Ardan gaped at him in confusion, as Cormac stormed from the café. After a long moment, Ardan returned to the kitchen and sat on one of the stools at the butcher-block table in the center of the room. He leaned into Deirdre, burying his head at her waist and sighing with relief as she stroked a hand through his hair and over his shoulders.

"It can't be as bad as all that, love," she murmured. After kissing him on the head, she set a few cookies in front of him with a glass of milk and winked.

He chuckled and bit into the molasses-flavored treat. "You always believe food will make it better."

"Yes, that or a cuddle," she said with a smile. She sobered when she saw he remained upset. "What happened? Does the customer want the day's soup?" She'd decided not to make soup today, believing few would be distraught to find it missing from the menu for one day.

Shaking his head, Ardan took a sip of milk and then swiped at his mouth with the back of his hand. "No. It was Cormac. Come to tell me that he's leaving. He believes it best for everyone if he's not in town."

Deirdre stilled what she was doing and gaped at him. "Why on earth would he believe that? Niamh has always relied on him." She shrugged. "At least, that's what she said. During the summer months, when his business is busy, and he barely has time to sleep, he's rarely around. But the rest of the year, he's an attentive uncle, or so it seems, and Maura loves her time with him."

Ardan nodded. "Aye." His gaze was distant. "There's so much I don't understand. Connor was a scoundrel. Was one since almost the moment he married Niamh. Loved firewater and cards more than he ever loved her." He paused as he saw the sadness in his wife's gaze. "But he never visited the Bordello. Not until that last night. Why was he there, lass?"

Deirdre hugged him close again, soothing him as much as she soothed herself by being in his embrace. "I don't know. But then I never truly knew the man. He wasn't even at our wedding long enough to dance with his wife." She shrugged. "A fact that didn't seem to bother Niamh."

"Niamh was like Maggie is now. Filled with light and joy and exuberance. And then she met Connor." He sighed. "I know we all failed her. But I don't know how we could have prevented her from marrying him." He whispered. "I feel so guilty because I rejoice that he is dead. That he can no longer provoke sadness or embarrassment in her gaze. And, all the while, she mourns."

Deirdre spoke in a low voice, as she kissed his head. "Do you think it might not be the same for her? That she is embarrassed because she feels as you? Perhaps she doesn't mourn as she believes she should, and she feels ashamed."

Ardan sighed and tugged Deirdre closer. "I wish she and my mum were reconciled. Mum knows what it feels like to rejoice at the burial of a spouse she loathes."

"Niamh will find her way, love," Deirdre soothed. "And, if there is justice in this world, she'll find her way to a good man this time."

"I dread telling my family Cormac's news, adding to Niamh's distress."

Deirdre nodded. "Perhaps tell your mum and da first, then decide when to tell Niamh."

~

A rdan watched Niamh nearly a week after the burial, and she was in as much of a daze as the night he, Kevin, and Da had had to inform her of her husband's death. Only Maura brought her out of her stupor. He approached her in the empty family kitchen in their parents' house and sat beside her. "Niamh?" he whispered.

She stared at him for a long moment, before blushing and ducking her head.

"Niamh?" he asked in confusion. "What's the matter?"

"I'm sorry, Ardan," she said in a barely audible voice. At his continued bafflement, she said, "For how I've treated you since this summer." Tears leaked out, and she blinked them away.

"None of that matters now, Niamh," he said. "All that's important is that you are safe and healthy and that you will be well again."

She flinched at his last statement and stared at him with a fleeting moment of panic. When he said nothing further, she relaxed. "My marriage wasn't happy for some time." At his nod, she flushed with apparent embarrassment. "I was envious of what you could have with Deirdre."

He clasped her hand. "There's nothing to apologize for, Niamh. You're human, like the rest of us." He sighed at the knock at the front door. "Don't run away," he murmured as he rose.

After thrusting the front door open, he frowned at the man on the step. "Sheriff."

"I need to speak with your sister, Niamh. Is she available?" Sheriff Wilcox asked. He was a bowlegged, barrel-chested man with a penetrating stare. Few had the temerity to cross him.

"Aye," Ardan said, as he opened the door wide and motioned him into the living room. He looked up the stairs to see his youngest brother, Bryan, staring down, wide-eyed. Ardan whispered at him, "Get Da," before following the sheriff and then leading him into the kitchen. Ardan smiled at his sister, as she sat up straight at the appearance of the lawman.

"Mr. Wilcox," she said. "I'm uncertain why you are seeking me out."

Sheriff Wilcox flushed and cleared his throat. "Would you like to speak with me in private, Mrs. Ahern?" he asked.

Niamh shared an alarmed look with her brother and shook her head. "No, I want my brother beside me." At the sound of someone entering the back door, she looked over her shoulder. "And my da."

Seamus entered the room and stood beside his seated daughter, placing a hand on her shoulder in support and solidarity. "Wilcox," he said in a deferential manner. He watched as the sheriff shifted his weight and rested his hand on the butt of his pistol. Although Seamus never allowed weapons in his house, he knew better than to ask the sheriff to leave his gun at the front door.

"Look. I have no desire to cause problems. Or to stir up a hornet's nest." He rubbed at his head. "But a man was killed, even if it was in a brothel." He flushed as he looked at Niamh. "I beg your pardon, ma'am."

Niamh held her shoulders back. "I understand the circumstances surrounding the death of my husband, Sheriff." She tilted her chin up and met his chagrined gaze with one of determination and pride.

Sheriff Wilcox cleared his throat, and his blush heightened. "I see. You understand he was drunk and on the verge of choking one of the Sirens to death?"

When Niamh blanched, Seamus swore. "Not every detail must be known, Sheriff."

Ignoring Niamh's father, Sheriff Wilcox took a step closer to Niamh and crouched, so he was at her eye level. "Mrs. Ahern, I understand your husband wasn't always … as considerate of you as he could have been." When Niamh merely stared at him with an impassive expression, he barreled on. "I've heard that he was a brute to you."

At her subtle nod, Ardan and Seamus hissed. "Why did you never say anythin'?" Ardan demanded.

Seamus stilled his approach to soothe his daughter at the severe glare the sheriff sent in his direction. "Now, Mrs. Ahern, some in town believe you encouraged your husband to a night of debauchery with the hope he wouldn't come home."

She stared at the sheriff mutinously. "My marriage with Connor was difficult," she whispered. "And I always prayed it would be more than it was. But I only would have harmed him if he had threatened our daughter, Maura." She shrugged. "He was mostly indifferent to her, and he gave me little reason to fear for her safety."

Seamus and Ardan stared at her, their jaws clenched tightly at all she said and at all that was implied.

The sheriff stood, heaving out a breath. "The matter stands that a man lost his life."

"I have no desire to press charges against anyone," Niamh proclaimed. "If Mr. Ezra had not intervened, an innocent woman would have died." She paused as the sheriff's eyes bulged at her description of a Bordello prostitute as an innocent woman. "And I doubt you would show such concern for her as you do for my husband."

Sheriff Wilcox blustered a moment, as she flushed with indignation. "I can see you are determined in your decision, ma'am." When Niamh nodded, he gave her a small bow. "Fine. For now, the matter is closed. However, if any other information comes to light, I will return."

Ardan escorted the sheriff to the front door and paused a moment. "Sir, what more could come to light? We already know what happened." He glowered as he considered the infamy his sister now lived under.

"We know he was killed. We know who did it. But I'm convinced there is more to this story than we understand." He took off his hat before slamming it back on his head again. "Why was he at the Bordello that night, drunk out of his mind?" He shook his head. "Connor Ahern was a drunk and a gambler, but he never visited the Bordello until the night he died. Something pushed him over the edge."

"For some men, no logical reason is needed for their dishonorable actions." Ardan watched the sheriff march away from the house, before returning to the kitchen. He saw his father, seated across from his sister with her hands in his. Ardan pulled out another chair and sat beside his da. "Niamh?" he whispered. "Why didn't you ever tell us how awful your marriage was?"

The fight left her, and she sat with her shoulders stooped. "What was I to say?" She laughed derisively at herself. "I ran away with him at Cow Island. I chose this life. Why should I complain about it?" She shook her head, as a sob escaped.

"Niamh," Ardan murmured, as a tear tracked down his cheek at the sight of his sister's misery. "I thought you mourned him."

"Promise me," Seamus whispered, "promise me, he never harmed you or Maura."

"I can't," she whispered brokenly, bowing her head and swiping at her cheeks. She looked away and saw Maura staring at her from the kitchen doorway. "My darling. You're awake."

"Mumma cry," Maura said, as she stumbled toward her mother in a half-sleep state, dragging a stuffed doll Seamus had given her.

"Mumma's fine," Niamh soothed, picking up her daughter and holding her close. "How could I be sad, holdin' you in my arms?" She forced a giggle as Maura patted her wet cheeks. Over her daughter's head, she sent a warning glance to her father and brother, effectively ending the conversation.

Ardan and Seamus shared a long look but nodded their agreement, as they had no desire to speak of unsettling topics in front of Maura.

That evening at supper, Ardan sat near his father. Ardan had already shared his concerns with Da that Cormac might leave, and Ardan knew his father had planned to speak with Cormac too. The younger boys had settled at the far end of the table, as they enjoyed telling tall tales. Niamh and Maura were beside Deirdre, while Kevin and Aileen were across from him and his mum. "Da," he said, in a voice loud enough for Kevin and Niamh to hear, "do you know if Cormac still plans to leave Fort Benton?"

Niamh's fork clattered to the tabletop, and she leaned forward to peer down the table at her eldest brother. "What, Ardan?"

He nodded at her. "Aye, he believes there's no reason for him to remain here. That he will spend the winter in Helena or Virginia City."

"But he'd return for the summer season," she argued. "We'd see him then."

Ardan shrugged. "I don't know. He seemed determined to run away from his memories here." He frowned as she flinched at his words. Ardan shared a frustrated look with his mother. "I reassured him that he was considered a part of our family, but he refused to believe me." He saw his mother let out a deep breath in disappointment and then watched as Niamh became distracted, helping her daughter, before entering a conversation with Aileen and Deirdre. Lowering his voice, Ardan spoke with his father and Kevin. "What did you learn, Da?"

Seamus studied his eldest daughter and then focused on Ardan. "I believe there is much we don't understand. Especially after the visitor today and all that was revealed." He clasped Mary's hand, as though silently asking her to wait until they were alone later for him to explain.

"I don't understand," Kevin said in a low voice. "What happened today?"

Sighing, Seamus said, "The sheriff called. Seemed he wanted Niamh to press charges, so he could arrest Ezra. But Niamh wouldn't." He rubbed at his temple and sat back in his chair.

"He implied the abuse showed the Siren was something Niamh would be familiar with," Ardan whispered.

Mary gasped, her gaze flying to her daughter, cuddling Maura. "No!"

Seamus nodded. "I very much fear I failed her, Mary." His gaze was filled with anger and self-recrimination. "But I refuse to believe she would want Cormac to leave. He's always been like another brother to her. She'd be lost without him."

Mary frowned at his words before nodding. "Aye, she'd be lost without him. But our Niamh needs time. Time to mourn and time to heal before she considers entering into another relationship. 'Twouldn't be fair to her or to the man if she were to jump straight into another marriage."

Seamus stilled as he considered Mary's words. "Cormac?" he whispered.

She smiled and patted his arm. "Aye, he's never been a brother to her, love."

Seamus shrugged, his gaze brightening at the thought of Cormac as a son-in-law. "I wish they could wait until they are ready, but sometimes we aren't given the luxury of waiting all the time we need before marryin' again." His brows furrowed, as though remembering his second wife, Colleen.

Mary shivered, as though recalling her marriage to her second husband, Francois, when she had thought Seamus had abandoned her. "I know."

"I will always pray Niamh's choice the second time is far superior to the first."

"If the man is Cormac, he will be," Mary murmured.

The following day dawned bright but cold. Even though only mid-October, winter was in the air. After searching for Cormac at his house, Niamh marched to the livery. Inside, she found him working on a harness in the tack room. "When would you have told me?" she demanded in a breathless voice, her hands on her hips as she stared at him. With flushed cheeks, wisps of hair floating around her face, and hazel eyes flashing with challenge, she stood with no evident fear in front of him.

His blue eyes shone with pride that he tried to conceal, as he lowered his gaze to focus on the harness in front of him. "I will come by, Niamh, if and when I decide to leave."

She let out a deep breath, collapsing onto a stool near him. "You aren't leaving," she breathed.

He shrugged, his large shoulders rolling, as though it were of no importance. "I haven't decided. When I do, I'll inform your family."

Niamh reached out, her hand gripping his and stilling his repetitive polishing of a bit of silver on the harness. "No, Cormac, tell me. Please." Her breath emerged as a shaky exhale. "I couldn't imagine not being able to talk with you. To not hear the truth from you."

He let out a mirthless chuckle. "That's rich. You haven't wanted to hear the truth from me for over two years." His alert gaze roved over hers, and he let out a deep breath, as though hoping it would ease him of his frustration and his despair. "Admit it."

She continued to hold her hand over his, as though unwittingly attempting to soothe him. "Please, Cormac."

He leaned closer to her, stilling his movement when he saw the flash of alarm in her beautiful hazel eyes. "I won't say any more. Not today." He paused, staring deeply into her tormented gaze. "Too much has been left unsaid between us, Niamh. But I care too much about you to ever wish to cause you a moment's worth of pain."

Niamh rose, yanking her hand back, severing all contact with him. "Thank you, Cormac." She spun on her heel and fought her inclination to race from the livery. She refused to examine if she were racing from her fear of Cormac leaving or her fear of all that Cormac meant to her. She fought shame that Connor had been right in his assessment of her. For, in all the ways that mattered, she had been unfaithful to her husband.

CHAPTER 3

The following day, Cormac rested on his back on his lumpy mattress in his cabin. Rain pinged off the roof, reminding him of long-distant days, when his father had praised their good fortune for the arrival of the spring rains and then cursed God and every Catholic Saint for the drenching rain that ruined their crops. Of his mother attempting to dry diapers in front of the fire, causing the room to steam and to heat to an uncomfortable level, all to swaddle her babes in dry cloth. Of his brothers placing metal tins in strategic places as the roof leaked, the *ping*ing noise keeping him awake long into the night. He sighed as he attempted to banish the memories of his youth.

Clamping his jaw tight, he ruthlessly battled remembering the worst of his childhood, instead focusing on the sound of the rain on the roof again. Memories of time he spent with Niamh overwhelmed him, like a stream bursting its riverbank. Swallowing, he let out a deep breath in an attempt to forget her too, but he knew that was futile. From the moment he'd seen her, he'd dreamed of her. Wanted to cherish her and to care for her. By a cruel twist of fate, he'd had to watch as his brother courted her.

"Damn you, Con," he muttered. The memory of his last fight with his brother was about to engulf him in grief, and he hit his fists on his mattress a few times. "Why did you have to choose Niamh?" However, deep inside, he knew. He knew it was to spite him. To prove him up again. To show that Connor was the elder and, thus, *better* brother.

Cormac's mind drifted to the first time he had seen Niamh on the deck of the steamboat as he and Connor had traveled up the Missouri in 1863. Few were brave enough to travel so far from civilization, as Montana Territory was still a politician's dream, and gold had just been discovered one year earlier. On the slow ride north on the nearly 2,500-mile journey that would take over two months, he feared Connor would wager away their money meant to start a business.

A brisk breeze blew, causing the seagulls to float in place, as they beat their wings at a frantic pace in their attempt to fly against the wind. When they allowed the wind to carry them away, they flew with tremendous speed out of sight. "Connor," Cormac said, as he clamped a hand on his hat, "you can't plan on spending every waking minute playing cards. You'll beggar us, and then we'll be destitute in a land where we know no one."

Connor rested with his back against the railing, his blond hair blowing in the wind and his brown eyes lit with the challenge inherent at the mention of a card game. "You're such a baby, Cormac. When will you learn to live a little? To experience life, rather than running around as though afraid what the next moment will bring you?" He slapped a hand on his brother's back and ambled away.

Swearing, Cormac kicked at the post holding up part of the railing and then gripped the railing, as though he wished he could rip it from its mooring. After taking a deep breath, he reminded himself that he had hidden away a portion of their funds, and he said a silent prayer that Connor never found it.

"You'll never solve your problems with a brother that way," said a soft, teasing, melodious voice. "With my brothers, I have to threaten them with bodily harm."

He gaped down at the small woman standing beside him, with her glossy auburn hair, and an impish gleam in her hazel eyes. "I can't imagine a slip of a woman could hurt a grown man. Unless they're midgets."

She laughed, a full-bodied and joyous sound, and he watched her, entranced, as her cheeks flushed and her hair fell from its pins. Swiping at her hair, she shook her head. "No, if you're smaller, or younger, you look for other ways to challenge a grown man." She leaned forward, as though revealing a tightly guarded secret. "I prefer wielding a cast iron skillet when necessary."

A laugh sputtered out, and he stared at her with incredulity. "How extraordinary."

She preened, standing a little taller and nodded. "Aye, I believe I am."

He leaned forward and listened intently as she spoke. "I detect an accent."

She stiffened, and the joy in her expression faded. After a long moment, where her gaze now focused on something on the horizon, she said, "I'm Irish. And, yes, I know all about the sentiment that Irish are not welcome here."

Shaking his head, Cormac smiled. "I've no complaint, miss." He raised an eyebrow to see if she would contradict him calling her miss and relaxed again when she merely watched him with curiosity. "My family is Irish too." He held out his hand and then shook his head, as he gave a stiff bow. "Cormac Ahern."

"Niamh O'Rourke. 'Tis a pleasure to meet you, Mr. Ahern." She looked over her shoulder and giggled. "I should go before one of my brothers looks for me. I'd hate for you to finish your journey too soon with a swim in the mighty Missouri." She giggled again as she spun and raced away.

Connor watched her, flummoxed and fascinated. After a long moment, he whispered to himself, "I'm going to marry that girl."

A knocking at his door brought him out of his reverie, and he rose to answer the call. "Yes?" he snapped, as he wrenched it open. "Niamh," he breathed. Without waiting for her to say anything, he pulled her inside. "You shouldn't be out in the rain."

Shivering, she moved to the small stove, huddling near its weak warmth. "Why didn't you build up your fire?" she asked, her teeth chattering.

"Wasn't much need with me alone in my cabin." He eased her to a chair, slung a blanket over her shoulders, and knelt in front of the stove to feed it a few pieces of wood. "There. You'll be warmer soon."

"I'll never be warm again," she whispered, staring at the stove and the hint of flames she could see behind the metal door. She flushed, but he couldn't determine if from a dawning warmth or from embarrassment.

"Niamh?" Cormac asked. "We've always been able to talk about everything with each other." He swore under his breath and rubbed at the muscles at the back of his neck. "Until this summer." He looked at her with a tortured expression. "You know we have to talk about it."

"No!" she gasped. "We don't. There's no need." She speared him with a severe glare, and he quieted any protest. "And, if you argue with me, I'll never speak with you again, Cormac Ahern, brother-in-law or not."

He froze, his breath emerging in pants at her threat. "Anything but that, Niamh. I couldn't bear it."

She closed her eyes and bent forward, hugging her arms around herself. "Just as I can't bear the gossip about town."

He frowned and gripped her hand. "What gossip ... ?" He paused as he swallowed the word he wished he could say. The unspoken endearment, *love*, hung between them, neither acknowledged nor acceptable. He ran a hand through his long brown hair, battling his frustration at the limitations of his relationship with Niamh.

"That Connor died because I was an unfaithful wife, who never loved him, and his unhappiness led him astray to his death."

Cormac gaped at her, the piece of wood he intended to replace in the woodbox missing its mark and clattering to the floor as he stared at her in shock. "You're serious."

"Aye," she whispered. "And it doesn't help that a lawyer's in town— stuck here because he didn't reach the steamboats to Saint Louis in time—who claims to have a will Connor wrote a week before he died."

Cormac collapsed into a chair, before scooting it over to face her. "Feck," he muttered, both at her news and because he now sat right beside the stove. "I feel like I'm on fire." He waited for her to giggle, for any hint of the vivacious young woman she had been to emerge. For any sign that she could still find humor in any situation. Instead she stared at him with a pinched, disappointed look. He moved his

34

chair away from the stove to sit beside her. "Do you have any idea what it said?"

She shook her head. "No, but the lawyer wants to meet with us tomorrow." She looked at Cormac. "Will you come?"

When he reached for her hand, she froze, a flash of fear in her gaze at his sudden movement, and he stilled. "I'm not Connor," he rasped. He waited for her to acknowledge that statement, but she sat beside him, her gaze glazed and a distant expression as she shook. "Look at me, Niamh."

When her head jerked up at his rough command, he swore again. "I won't hurt you. I promise."

She shook her head. "You're wrong. All men do. Everyone does. I'm not worthy of lasting respect or love." She pushed herself from her chair. "Be at Da's house at eleven."

"Niamh," he called out, but she ran into the rain, the door clattering shut after her. "Oh, my love," he whispered. "How I yearn to soothe you and to prove you wrong."

He collapsed onto his bed again, his mind filled with images of Niamh now. Although only two and a half years had passed since he had met her, it seemed as though she had aged a decade. Gone was the woman filled with laughter, curiosity, and an irrepressible joy. How he longed to help her rediscover the woman she was before life had betrayed her.

The next day Niamh sat in numb silence, as she awaited the arrival of Cormac and the lawyer. Aileen and Deirdre had insisted on watching Maura, and Niamh longed to hold her daughter in her arms. She found she needed comforting as much as she would like to comfort her daughter. At the knock on the front door, she curled into herself and ignored the worried looks shared by her father and her two eldest brothers, Ardan and Kevin.

After a moment Da led the lawyer into the rear kitchen. Her impression of him did not improve upon her second meeting. He walked with a swagger and looked around the simple, homey kitchen, as though it were fit only for beggars, not the most prominent family in Fort Benton. Standing beside her father and Ardan, he had to peer up at them, as he was a good six inches shorter than either of them. The buttons of his teal silk waistcoat strained over what she suspected was his ever-expanding paunch, and a gold watch hung from a pocket. With a hand in one pocket, he rocked on his heels, as though king of all he surveyed.

"You are very welcome, I'm sure," Seamus said, pointing to the table nearby, with none of the customary warmth in his voice. Rather than offer him coffee or tea, he motioned for the man to sit at the kitchen table.

"You expect me to conduct important business in the kitchen?" the lawyer asked. "I am Uriah Chaffee, Esquire, of the law, and I would have thought you could find a more suitable place for our discussion."

Seamus smiled, although his eyes shone with distaste. "In our family, there is no better place to discuss our most important concerns. Sit." His tone brooked no argument, and the lawyer sat at a chair near the end of the table, although he seemed to have the sense not to choose Seamus's customary seat at the head of the table.

At a clatter on the back step, Niamh looked to the door and relaxed slightly at the sight of Cormac. "You came," she breathed.

With a nod, he looked around the room, shaking the hands of the men present, although he appeared to fight a grimace at having to clasp the lawyer's hand. He sat beside Niamh and waited with a pointed look for the lawyer to begin spouting his legal jargon.

Seamus held up a hand, preventing Mr. Chaffee from speaking. "Now, Mr. Chaffee. I understand you are a man of expensive words, but we are more simple people. I'd appreciate it if you spoke in clear terms about what you came to discuss today."

Niamh watched as her eldest brother, Ardan, fought a smile at their father's tactics. Seamus always portrayed himself as a simple man from a poor land, misleading those around him into believing they could outwit him, due to his perceived ignorance and lack of intelligence. Nine times out of ten, Seamus saw through their schemes and tricked them.

Mr. Chaffee puffed out his chest, like a rooster about to crow, and she ducked her head at her misfortune that Connor had visited this man. That this man had been stranded in Fort Benton for the winter. Interrupting her thoughts, she froze as Cormac gripped her hand under the table.

"Thank you, Mr. O'Rourke. I always suspected you were a man of reason and intelligence. As you know, I am a highly educated man, who has been trapped in this backwater town due to the nefarious information of the deceitful Dunmore. How that man is free to walk the streets and to work with customers is beyond me. Why, if I hadn't had the sense to ensure ..."

"Mr. Chaffee," Seamus snapped. "The matter at hand." He tapped his index finger on the kitchen table.

"Of course, of course," Mr. Chaffee said, extracting a sheaf of papers from a small satchel at his side. "I had the good fortune of speaking with Mr. Connor Ahern the day before he died. And might I add, he was a most unhappy man." He looked at Niamh with condemnation, as he made a *tsk*ing noise. "No man likes to be made aware of his wife's perfidy."

Ardan slammed his hand on the table. "Mr. Chaffee, the will."

"Look at her, sitting beside the man, as brazen as any Siren at the Bordello." Mr. Chaffee waved his hand at Niamh, as she sank into herself, trying to disappear from view.

"If you don't cease your comments about Mrs. Ahern, you won't be speakin' much longer," Cormac said in a low menacing voice. "She is a good and respectable woman, and you'd do well to remember it." He glared at Mr. Chaffee when he acted as though to argue with Cormac's mandate for silence on the topic of Niamh. "Now, what did my brother write in that fancy document?"

Mr. Chaffee cleared his throat and opened up the papers, sitting stiffly and glaring at the assembled people at the table as though he were a wronged man. When he realized no one would agree with him and his assertions, he cleared his throat and gave the papers a little shake. "Now, if you will allow me to complete my task, I must read this in its entirety. Consider me as though I am speaking for your late murdered husband, for whom you have shown far too little sorrow, Mrs. Ahern, and for whom you refuse justice to avenge." He began to read in a clear voice. *"I, Connor Ahern, have but one desire. To make a final will and testament. I have no desire to leave anything to my so-called wife, Niamh O'Rourke Ahern. She deserves nothing. She is nothing to me. And she knows why."*

Mr. Chaffee lowered the paper, staring for a long moment at Niamh, who sat in ashen silence. After the pregnant pause, where his eyes gleamed with speculation as he looked at the shocked expressions of those present, he continued. *"My only wish is to leave the little I can claim as mine to my daughter, Maura. She is the one pure light in my life, and I would ensure she is cared for. With that in mind, I leave all my earthly goods in trust with Nora Flaherty. As such, Nora Flaherty is to be guardian of my daughter in the event of my unfortunate and untimely demise. My so-called wife cannot be trusted in the upbringing of my precious daughter."*

"Bastard!" Ardan roared as he slammed his hand on the table and rose. "Those are filthy lies and can't be enforced."

Mr. Chaffee held up the papers, a delighted gleam in his eye. "Oh, but it can be. And it should be. A father's dying wish should never be ignored." He stared at Niamh with glee. "I have a meeting arranged with the sheriff this afternoon."

"No," Niamh rasped, as she fell forward, her head nearly hitting the tabletop, losing all her strength. "You can't take my baby from me." Tears spilled from her eyes, and she looked at her father and brothers in supplication. "Please, anything to save her. Anything."

Cormac squeezed her hand and whispered softly for only her to hear, "Anything?"

At her subtle nod, he sighed. "My brother had no right to assign a guardian for Maura." He stared with lethal intensity at the lawyer, who appeared to be relishing their misery. "First, I doubt you have any legal foothold in the Territory." At the lawyer's attempt at bluster, Cormac glared him into silence again. "For all we know, you're a charlatan with no skills, other than an ability to spout hundred-dollar words and feast on misery."

"Now, you listen here, young man—"

Cormac continued to speak, ignoring the lawyer's protest. "No, I will not listen to another vile thing you have to say. And I refuse for you to separate *my* daughter from her mother."

CHAPTER 4

A deafening silence filled the room as Ardan gaped at them, Kevin's jaw dropped open, and Seamus swore. "Feck," he said, as he rose and began to pace. "How could you, lad?" Seamus snapped at Cormac. His bluster covered Niamh's gasp of shock.

When Cormac shrugged and stared placidly at the O'Rourke men, it was as though he had added fuel to her father's ire. "You know I've always loved Niamh."

"Like a sister," Seamus roared. "Never like a ... like a ..." He broke off as he spun away to stare out the window.

Ardan looked at the lawyer. "Now that we know Maura's parentage is in doubt, I'm certain that places Connor's decree in doubt too."

"No," Mr. Chaffee said, unable to hide a giggle of amusement. "It only makes me more delighted that I missed that steamboat. Nothing in Saint Louis would have proven half as entertaining." He preened as he ran a hand over his silk waistcoat. "Mr. Ahern, Mr. *Connor* Ahern," he said, as though clarifying an important detail, "clearly believed himself to be the father. And, as he was the one married to Mrs. Ahern at the time, although I would use that term lightly," he said, as he sniffed with disdain in Niamh's direction, "he is legally acknowledged as the child's father. Thus, his wishes are the wishes to be followed."

"No one in this town will allow you to separate Maura from Niamh," Cormac said with a low growl.

"I think plenty will find it entertaining to see an O'Rourke residing in the Bordello. To see that the next generation will have a Madam for tutelage." He slipped his papers into his satchel and rose. "If you will excuse me, I have other townsfolk I must visit today." He sauntered from the room, with the O'Rourkes sitting in stunned silence.

"Da," Niamh whispered.

"No, Niamh, not now," Seamus whispered. "Everyone out." He turned to stare with mortal hatred at Cormac. "Except you. You remain."

"Da," Ardan attempted to soothe Seamus, but his father shook his head. When Seamus again bellowed, "Out!" Ardan eased an arm around Niamh's shoulders and urged her from the kitchen to the front living room.

Although the newly constructed door to the kitchen was rarely closed, Seamus slammed it shut behind his departing children. He stood tall, with the righteous indignation of a wronged father, as he stared at the man who he thought he could trust. "How dare you?"

Cormac rose, matching Seamus for height and rage. "I dared because I truly love your daughter. Unlike my brother."

"You defiled her," Seamus rasped, his breath sawing in and out of him, as though he had just run a race.

"My loving your daughter would never tarnish her." He waited as the unspoken words, *unlike Connor's love*, reverberated through the room. Closing his eyes, Cormac sighed. "I wish I had," he murmured. He opened his eyes to gaze at Seamus. "I wish I had."

At the repeated words, Seamus relaxed and gazed at Cormac. "I don't understand, lad. What are you and Niamh playing at?" He paused. "I've always known how much you care for her."

"No, you haven't," Cormac said with a bitter smile. "You've always assumed I love her like I would a sister." He paused. "Do you know what I said to myself right after I met her?" When Seamus motioned for him to continue speaking, Cormac whispered, "I promised myself I would marry her someday. Instead she married Connor."

"*Ahh*, lad," Seamus breathed.

"I know you are friends with Madam Nora. And I have no doubt she would treat Maura well. But Maura has suffered enough confusion in her young life. She needs her mother." He closed his tormented sky-blue eyes. "And there's nothing I wouldn't do to ensure Niamh has whatever and whomever she needs to find peace again."

Gripping Cormac's shoulders, Seamus squeezed them so hard that Cormac's hands became numb. "You promise nothing untoward occurred between you and Niamh?"

Cormac sighed. "Nothing that would cause Maura to be mine, no."

Seamus stilled as he considered Cormac's evasive answer and then swore. "Feck, this is more complicated than I thought." He ran a hand over his temple, as he always did when he was upset about something. "You do realize you've just caused Niamh to be subjected to even more gossip? Her husband dyin' in the Bordello wasn't enough for her to suffer, aye?"

"She had already suffered plenty more," Cormac snapped and then grimaced at what he had inadvertently revealed.

"And what is that, lad?" Seamus stood in front of Cormac, preventing him from retreating. "What exactly did my Niamh endure besides the disillusionment of marrying a lazy man?"

Cormac clamped his jaw shut. "I promised," he hissed. "I can't tell you."

Seamus saw the torment in the young man's eyes, and his shoulders stooped. "'Tis why you had such a distance between you and Connor at the end. Because you knew something that upset you." He spoke in a voice barely audible, as though, by speaking the words, it made them real. Something he could not stand to be true. "That he had a penchant for treating his wife with the violence he showed the Siren."

Cormac's eyes gleamed with pain as he nodded subtly.

"Oh, my poor wee babe," Seamus rasped, his startling blue eyes filling with tears. "Brother or no, if he were alive today, I'd rip him limb from limb."

"As he would deserve." Cormac ducked his head. "I failed her, sir, and she won't accept my apology. I'm so sorry."

Seamus gripped his shoulders again and let out a heaving breath. "From now on, we do what we must to protect her, lad. Whatever we must."

"Aye," Cormac said. He allowed Seamus to pull him in for a tight embrace, before he backed away. "Niamh will be angry with me."

"She's irate with the world," her father argued. "Give her time." He cleared his throat. "For, when a few months have passed, you do understand you'll have to marry. After such a proclamation to a man like Chaffee, you have to marry my Niamh."

Cormac froze. "I won't force her to do anything, sir."

"She outwitted me the first time when she raced away with your brother, but she won't a second. She'll marry you and be damn glad of it."

~

Niamh allowed Ardan to ease her onto the sofa, her gaze unfocused as an unremitting shaking began. Images of her beautiful Maura filled her mind. Her smile. Her chortle when she did something new. Her delight at learning to walk and then to run. The soft sound of her sweet voice calling her "Mumma." Niamh bent forward, burying her face in her wool skirts as a sob burst forth.

Ardan sat on one side of her and Kevin the other. A hand caressed her back, and Ardan said in a soothing, yet determined voice, "Don't worry, Niamh. We'll never allow anyone to take Maura away."

"But what if it's the law?" she stuttered out. "What if I have no rights?"

"You're her mother. Of course you have rights," Kevin snapped. "This is just that bastard's attempt to continue to control you and to hurt you, even from the grave."

Niamh shuddered and sniffled. "I knew he detested me, but I never imagined he'd make our discord public."

With a hesitant voice, Ardan asked, "Did he have reason to be angry with you and Cormac?"

Niamh rose, separating herself from her brothers and any comfort they had attempted to offer her. "No!" She flushed. "Not like Cormac insinuated in there." After yanking a handkerchief from her pocket, she scrubbed at her face. "I promised myself I'd never cry again over Connor." She shook her head as she clamped her jaw shut.

"You're not crying over him," Kevin said. "You're crying over what he's trying to do to you. Those are very different things, Niamh." He tilted his head to one side, as his inquisitive hazel eyes studied her. "You never showed much remorse at the loss of your husband."

Flinching, Niamh turned away to study the bare wall. "If you had married such a person, I doubt you would have acted much differently." She wrapped an arm around her body, anchoring her hand on her shoulder. "Cormac and I did nothing to cause either of us any shame." She turned around in time to see her brothers share a long look. "You don't believe me, do you?"

Ardan rose, his blue eyes shining with confusion and sincerity. "Why would a man we know to be honorable, who was also loyal to his brother, proclaim such a thing if it were a lie? He'd have to be ..." He broke off, as though a thought he didn't care to voice just came to him.

"He's loyal to me and Maura too. And we're still alive, while Connor's dead. After Connor dishonored our wedding vows at the Bordello." Her voice broke.

"Don't you see that you and Cormac have just taken away any sympathy the townsfolk might have had for you by this declaration? That they'll now believe Connor was justified in seeking out comfort at the Bordello? And equally justified for his rage?" Ardan said.

Niamh swayed, and Kevin gripped her arm, easing her to the sofa. "I just wanted to find a way to keep Maura safe. To keep her with me." Her voice broke once more. "I didn't care what Cormac said."

Kevin gripped her hand, as her tears coursed down her cheeks and she sat in silent misery. "You need to consider why an honorable man, loyal to his brother, would speak out on your behalf, Niamh. And then determine what you are willing to do to repay such devotion."

~

C ormac slipped from the O'Rourke house, overwhelmed after the meeting with the lawyer and unwilling to see Niamh again so soon. To keep himself busy during the off-season months, he worked with the livery owner, repairing tack, mucking out stalls, and doing any other task that needed to be done. Generally his wages consisted of a warm meal and a never-ending pot of coffee, which suited him. He had no desire for riches, unlike his brother, who always believed he would strike it rich at the gambling tables. Or by marrying an heiress.

After mucking out two stalls, Cormac moved to the tack room. Frowning at finding most of it in good shape, he decided to polish it. Again. Anything to keep busy. Although he doubted her family had heard Niamh's gasp of dismay at his proclamation, it had pierced his soul. The sound of her distress as he had attempted to aid her had nearly unmanned him. With a groan, he slammed the now shiny bridle onto the counter and lowered his head. What more could he do to show her his love? Were constancy and devotion no longer desirable? Or so easily taken for granted?

He closed his eyes, as Seamus's proclamation that he would marry Niamh filled him with joy and trepidation. For he wanted Niamh to choose to marry him. To find delight at the prospect in marrying him. Not to feel trapped into marriage to escape scandal. Not a second time.

He sighed as the scene from over two years ago played out in his mind. A scene he had rewritten a thousand times but had never emerged with him as the groom.

Cormac sat in the stagecoach, his mind reeling with implications, as Connor crowed with glee.

"There's my lass. Independent. Not searching for her father's approval."

46

Connor threw an arm over Niamh's shoulder, ignoring his brother's grunt as his hand hit Cormac in the head in the tight stagecoach where six were crammed inside for the journey to Fort Benton from Cow Island, where the steamboat had docked. "Finally we will have time alone together."

Cormac peered around Niamh to gape at his brother. "Connor, you can't—"

Connor glared him into silence. "None of your brothers or your father will be able to keep us apart now, my little love."

Scowling, Cormac watched as Niamh gazed at Connor, as though he hung the stars and the moon. All through the long, uncomfortable journey, Cormac prayed Niamh would come to her senses. That she would see his brother's insincerity. After arriving in Fort Benton, and with Connor aware the O'Rourke men would be in hot pursuit, Cormac knew Connor would attempt to seduce Niamh.

"Niamh," Cormac gasped, as he raced to catch up to her, after she had exited the bathhouse with a spring in her step. He'd kept watch at the door, refusing admittance to any man so she was ensured privacy. His breath caught as her auburn hair hung loose around her shoulders, cascading down her back as it dried.

Her rosy cheeks and skin clean from the mud and the days' worth of travel, she gazed at him with anticipation and delight in her eyes.

"Don't do anything rash."

"I've known him a few months now, Cormac," she said, as she patted his hand, as though he were an old man who needed soothing. "Why would you believe I'm acting in a reckless manner?"

He flushed with anger. "Because you raced away with him in defiance of your father's wishes. Because you know you'll have to marry him if you agree to his plans for you tonight." His cheeks reddened further. "You deserve better, Niamh."

Shaking her head in disappointment, she furrowed her brows as she studied him. "How can you say that about your own brother? Shouldn't you want him to marry me?" Taking a step forward, she tapped him in his chest with her finger. "Why am I not good enough for him?"

"No, that's not what I mean." His sky-blue eyes filled with panic. "He's promised to another. He should stay true to her."

Niamh rolled her eyes and then shrugged. "Connor explained it all to me, Cormac. Why should he be bound to a woman he may never see again? She doesn't have the adventurous nature to travel here. Besides," she said, as she looked around the tiny town, "why shouldn't I marry him? He's a fine man, and it's not as though I'd want to marry anyone else here."

He paled and backed up a step. "No, of course not," he rasped. "I beg your pardon." He watched as she scurried away for her rendezvous with his brother.

The following morning, her father and brothers arrived, all of them crammed into and onto a stagecoach. After one look at Niamh, her father had sworn out loud with no apologies and then found a pastor to marry her to his brother. Although Seamus would have preferred a priest, he had a practical nature and had accepted any man of the cloth to save his daughter's tattered reputation.

As Cormac stood beside Connor, watching Niamh approach in the patched-together ceremony, Cormac marveled at the joy, wonder, and relief in her gaze as she walked toward Connor. As his hopes turned to ash, Cormac watched his brother marry the woman of his dreams.

That evening, a subdued O'Rourke family sat around the kitchen table. Rather than the customary boisterous group with lively discussions, all conversations were in muted voices, and few laughed or smiled. Although the younger siblings did not understand what had occurred that day, when the lawyer had called, they understood the news had not been well received.

At the knock on the back door, Seamus rose. Although Mary had cooked his favorite foods, he had not had an appetite for most of it. "Whoever is calling had better be civil," he muttered to Mary. "Yes," he barked as he tugged open the door. "Madam," he breathed. "I had hoped we had a little time before you called."

"May I come in, Seamus?" she asked, as she stood on the back stoop. "Or must I call you *Mr. O'Rourke?*" Her mouth twitched with amusement, as she and Seamus had had a strong friendship since

Seamus's arrival in Fort Benton two and a half years ago. They had truly been friends, never lovers, as he had sought out her counsel and her companionship after the death of his second wife and before the return of Mary.

"Of course," he said. He stepped backward, accepting her black cloak, coated in a fine mist. After hanging it by the fire to dry, he motioned for her to join them at the table, where all conversation had halted at her appearance. "I would like to introduce Ma—Nora Flaherty," Seamus said, faltering as he was about to call her *Madam*. "She is very welcome." He sent a beseeching look in Mary's direction and heaved out a sigh of relief as his stalwart wife rose and opened her arms to embrace the Madam, as though they were long-lost friends.

"Nora, 'tis lovely to see you," Mary said. "Please, won't you join us for dinner?"

"Oh, I couldn't, but thank you." She sat in a chair near Seamus, Mary, and Niamh, her gaze roving over the numerous children staring at her. "I had never fully imagined what having twelve children was like."

"This is a quiet evening. Three of the lads are missin', as they are in Saint Louis," Seamus said, as he waved at the table. "An' Ardan and Deirdre are at the café tonight."

"Imagine," Nora murmured, as she looked at the crowded table with wonder. She smiled her thanks as Mary set a cup of tea in front of her. After adding milk and sugar, Nora spoke in a soft voice. "Forgive me for interrupting, but I received an interesting visitor today and did not want to wait before speaking with you. I had no desire for further rumors to spread."

Seamus gave a nearly imperceptible nod. "Aye." He looked at his youngest sons, chatting but no longer eating. "Lads, we need privacy." He smiled his thanks as they rose, leaving the kitchen. "You too, Maggie." He watched as his youngest daughter flushed with embarrassment and disappointment but obeyed his instructions, taking wee Maura with her.

At his glance, Mary closed the door to the kitchen he'd had

installed a few months before. "Will you wait to speak until we're all here?" After the Madam shrugged her agreement, Seamus spoke with Kevin. "Fetch Ardan and Cormac."

After the younger siblings were settled away from the kitchen, and Ardan, Deirdre, and Cormac were present, Seamus stared at the Madam. "Nora, I never expected to find you on my doorstep."

She smiled ruefully. "And I never expected to be involved in a tug of war between a dead man and his disgruntled wife, Seamus." She sighed as she took a sip of tea. "Although I've always been intrigued by parenthood, it's forever been in a remote way one considers events never destined to occur. I've known that, with my lifestyle, I would not have a child." She looked at Niamh, sitting in silent misery across the table from her, with her shoulders stooped and chin lowered. "Fight, girl."

Niamh's head jerked up, and she stared at Nora in confusion. "I don't know what you mean."

"Fight back. You have the word of a renegade lawyer, claiming he spoke with your husband. How do any of us know this man tells the truth?" She paused as she looked around the room at the O'Rourkes.

"What reason does he have to lie?" Cormac asked. He sat beside Niamh, as though unable to sit anywhere else but next to her.

Mary studied the Madam. "You're far more intelligent than you like the men who visit your establishment to know, aren't you?" At the Madam's diffident shrug, Mary smiled.

"Men will always believe a woman his inferior because we aren't as physically strong," Nora said with a roll of her eyes. "They've yet to learn that a strategy and the execution of that strategy can be far more potent a foe." She smiled slyly before taking another sip of tea.

Seamus shared a long look with Mary and then focused on the Madam. "What do you know, lass?"

Nora ran a hand over her fine red satin dress, cut to highlight her figure. "I know the man enjoys provoking discord. He likes intrigue. And that he was nearly strung up in Virginia City for false claims about a man's wife." She looked around the table as she shrugged again.

After a long pause as those at the table considered all she said, Cormac asked, "Why would he make false claims about Connor and Niamh? What would he hope to gain?"

Nora rolled her eyes and spoke in a slow voice, as though explaining to a child. "He's like your brother." When Cormac flushed, Nora continued. "He sees a vulnerable woman and hopes to exploit the situation. However, he miscalculated."

"What do you mean?" Seamus asked, waving at Cormac to calm as he focused on Nora.

Staring at them all with blatant fascination, Nora asked, "Did any of you ask to read the so-called will? To review it yourselves?" At their shakes of their heads, Nora said, "Well, I did. And I happened to have an unfortunate accident with a teacup as I reviewed it. The poor man was most distressed that his hard work was blemished by my fine Ceylon tea, although I assured him there would be nothing more than a slight discoloration to his long-winded will. I wonder if he is paid by the word." She smiled like a cat that had just found a bowl of cream. "I imagine he'll be disappointed to discover he has a sheet from my ledger, highlighting my increased need for satin and lace, rather than the so-called will, when he looks over his paperwork."

"Why?" Mary asked, as she watched Nora open her small bag. "Why help us in this manner?"

Nora paused in extracting a few sheets that appeared tea stained. "I will always consider Seamus a friend, and I will always admire his loyalty to family." Her gaze flickered to Aileen. "Mrs. Aileen is a good friend and a hard worker who doesn't look at my girls, *or me*, as though we are inferior to her. We are still people to her." She paused, her gaze fixed on Mary. "And you've treated me like a respected guest since I arrived in your home. You even invited me to dinner."

"If we hadn't, would you have shared those papers with us?" Mary asked.

"I'm uncertain," Nora whispered. "One does become tired of being deemed unworthy and invisible." She shrugged and opened the sheaf of papers. "But none of that matters as I was welcomed. And you've all acted with honor. Unlike the lawyer."

"What does the will say, lass?" Seamus asked, canting forward. He noted everyone at the table leaned forward too.

Flushing for the first time, Nora said in a terse voice, "The first part is unflattering to Mrs. Ahern, and I have no wish to say such horrible things." She looked around the table at the glowers on the men's faces and the shame in Niamh's, and she sighed. "I imagine Mr. Chaffee took great joy in reading that section."

At Seamus's *aye*, Nora focused on the next section. "It does say that I am to be Maura Ahern's guardian. However, there are stipulations. And I worry those stipulations were not discussed with you."

Niamh spoke, her hand reaching forward to grab the paper. "No. He said I had to give up my daughter and acted as though there were nothing more to it." Her gaze roved over the paper, and she paled. "Why? Why would Connor write such a thing?"

Cormac pulled the paper from Niamh's hold, his gaze flying over the page as he flushed and then swore softly. After a moment, he swallowed and then took a deep breath. "I know you believe this is not my brother's will, but it is. He was spiteful and mean when he felt he'd been betrayed. Or when someone crossed him. And he believed Niamh had done both."

Nora shook her head in confusion. "Why would he think his stipulation a punishment?"

"He hated me," Niamh whispered. "And he believed any man who had to marry me would be as miserable as he believed himself miserable."

"Niamh," Mary whispered, her eyes glistening as she beheld her daughter's desolation. "You know that's a blatant lie, love."

"You left," Niamh breathed. "Why should my husband have loved me any more than you did?" She ignored her mother's indrawn breath of pain at her words.

"Niamh," Seamus said in his deep voice, warning Niamh to not further upset her mother. Turning to Cormac, he asked, "What does the condition say?"

"It states '*As is well-known in the town of Fort Benton, Niamh Ahern is an unfit mother. Rarely can she care for our daughter without the assistance of a family member. Always does she put her desire to work before the needs of her child, due to her selfish yearning to be as successful as her pathetic family. To prove her love, and to deserve the right to raise my daughter, she must marry again. For she should never have the chance to ruin my child's life by raising her alone to mold into an image of herself, a heartless woman unfamiliar with the concepts of love, honor, or devotion."*

"Bastard," Ardan rasped and then muttered his apologies to his mother. "How dare he insinuate you are a bad mother?"

"Or that you work because you are trying to compete with your family?" Deirdre said. "We all know it's because he frittered away every penny he ever earned at the gambling table and at the saloon."

Niamh sat in stunned silence. "I wanted a little something for Maura that wasn't given to us by you, Da. I'm paying for my pride."

"No, my darlin' daughter, no," Seamus said, as he reached forward to grab her hand. "You aren't. And you won't. You know what you must do. Marry again. Turn this farce of a will to your advantage. Marry a good man this time."

"No such man exists," she whispered.

"Niamh," Cormac rasped, as he recoiled from her side. He abruptly rose and stepped around the table. "I thank you, Nora, for your help tonight. You aided in answering questions I had."

Nora gazed at him with abject sadness and disappointment. "I wish you didn't have to leave."

Cormac shook his head and backed away. "Oh, but I do," he whispered, looking at Niamh with torment in his gaze. He paused, as though waiting for Niamh to protest his abrupt departure, but she refused to look in his direction or to speak. "I do." He spun and fled from the room.

Nora looked at Niamh and sighed. "That was foolish, girl." When everyone else remained quiet, Nora rose. "For now, I will leave you. However, Niamh, I recommend you attempt to see sense. Mr. Chaffee will be only too glad to attempt to ruin your life by tearing your daughter away from you if you don't marry and marry soon."

After Nora had left, Seamus motioned for everyone else present to remain seated. He stared long and hard at his daughter, who remained quiet. Mary sat beside him, quivering as she attempted to quell her sobs.

Finally Ardan burst out, "How could you, Niamh?" His blue eyes gleamed with impassioned confusion. "How could you treat the man who has always stood by you with such contempt?"

"You don't understand," Niamh whispered, her head bowed, her hands clutched together tightly.

"Make us," Kevin demanded.

Deirdre made a noise of distress and shook her head. "No, Ardan. Kevin. No." She spoke in a low, soothing tone, her deep smoky voice filled with concern. "He—Cormac—has to do with why you were sick in the summer, doesn't he?"

Niamh stared at her in horror, her eyes widened as she became ashen in color. "How do you know?"

Deirdre closed her eyes. "I don't know much," she said, as she met her husband's disappointed gaze. "And I did not betray you, Ardan. Niamh didn't say anything, but I had a suspicion that things were not going well with Connor. As did everyone else."

Seamus rapped his fingers on the table. "What matters is that you make peace with Cormac. And that he fulfills his brother's wishes so that you never have to fear losing Maura." He spoke in a gentle tone. "Your daughter is important, Niamh."

Niamh jerked, as though her father had struck her, and stumbled to her feet. "Of course. Maura must be protected. I'm of little consequence in all this." She raced from the room, slamming the kitchen door shut behind her.

"Feck," Seamus whispered. "I'll go to her when she's calmed down." He looked at his sons. "Keep an eye out for that Chaffee. He finds too great a joy in another's sorrow and must never be trusted." With that, he eased Mary up and helped her upstairs to soothe her.

∽

Cormac stormed out of the O'Rourke house. Uncertain of his destination, he walked for minutes, gasping and then swearing softly as he stood at the temporary marker for his brother. Staring at the poorly carved wooden inscription, he glared at it.

CA
1831–1865

"Damn you, Connor," he whispered. "Damn you for everything you did to her. For everything you failed to do. For what you continue to do to her from the grave." He closed his eyes, as he attempted to calm his anger, but a deep-seated rage had taken root, and he worried it would never be calmed.

"You knew I loved her and took joy in stealing her from me. Why would a brother act in such a way?" He fell to his knees, as he continued to rant at his brother. "I swore, after you married, that I wouldn't spend time with you. That I would live a life separate from you."

He bent forward, beating his hands on the ground. "But you found a way to entice me to spend time with you. With her. You shoved salt in the wound of my disappointment every time you kissed her in front of me. Every time you taunted me with Maura. Every time you put that look of resignation and desolation in her gaze."

He swiped at his eyes, smearing dirt as he rubbed away tears. "You were my only living family, Connor." He paused. "I'll never forgive you for what you did in August. Never."

Seamus held Mary in his arms as she sobbed. He did not attempt any false words to soothe her as he knew the reality of the situation would prove a lie to anything he said. Although he loved Niamh, he had trouble tempering his anger with her and her treatment of her mother. How could she not know how Mary had suffered after losing them? That their nearly eighteen years of separation had haunted Mary as it had all of them?

Mary's tears slowly abated, but she continued to cling to him as her breaths stuttered in and out of her. "Don't let me go," she pleaded with her husband.

"Never, *a ghrá*," he whispered. "My love, I would have spared you that if I could."

"She will never forgive me," Mary cried, her fingers digging into his back.

"*Shh*, love, she will. Niamh's dealing with loss and fear, and she's striking out at all those who are close to her. She's yet to make her peace with Ardan after this summer, although they have formed a sort of truce."

"She doesn't lash out at you," Mary said and then flushed at her petulant tone. "I'm sorry, darling. I'd never want you to suffer as I am."

Seamus cupped her face and tilted it up so he could look deeply into her eyes. "Don't you understand, Mary, how I would endure all this pain for you if I could? It's torture for me to see you suffer."

"Oh, Shay," she cried, as she rested her head on his chest. "All I want to do is hold her close and cherish her as her mother. But she won't let me. She wants nothing to do with me. And I can't force her to accept me back into her life."

Seamus sat in quiet contemplation as he listened to the sounds of his house. His boys chattering downstairs. Maggie soothing an upset Maura. The nearly indiscernible sobs he knew were Niamh's, as she cried herself to sleep in her room. "Soon, my love, soon, your daughter will need you. And I trust you will prove as generous with your love as you have always. For she needs you as much as any of us. Perhaps more."

"Oh, Shay, I pray for that every night," his wife murmured, as she fought sleep in his arms.

When he knew she had tumbled into sleep, he rested her on the bed, running a hand over her silky hair and giving thanks once more that his beloved Mary had been returned to them.

CHAPTER 5

The following morning, Niamh left Maura with her aunt Aileen, with her sister-in-law's promise that she would not bring her daughter anywhere near the Bordello. Niamh wrapped a warm cloak around her and set out for a walk. She knew she couldn't walk far, as she had no desire to climb up the large bluffs that bracketed the backside of the town. However, she needed to escape the stifling disapproval in her father's house.

Once outside, she paused to breathe deeply of the crisp fall air. A hawk soared overhead, swooping up and down as it searched for prey. Pausing a short distance from town, she closed her eyes, tilting her head up to the sun, basking in its warmth. Too soon, the cool days of fall would give way to winter.

Unbidden, images of Connor flooded her mind. A smirk. A condescending look. A derisive comment about her attempt to cook a different meal. His snide, disdainful disregard for her ideas. His gaze filled with boredom and disappointment as he looked at her. His indifference as he ignored Maura. Niamh shivered, crossing her arms over her chest.

Just as suddenly, she thought of Cormac. Always smiling. His gaze filled with faith every time he looked at her. Encouraging her to do what she thought she couldn't do. Believing her ideas had merit as he listened to her. His laughter as he found joy in all she did. His wonder at Maura as she grew.

With a shudder, she whispered to herself, "He's not Connor." Although she instinctively knew that, she had battled a deep fear that the brothers were more alike than she had wanted to admit to herself. That Cormac would be just like Connor and would change into a man she didn't recognize if she were to marry him. Or perhaps that her judgment was irrevocably flawed because she had chosen Connor rather than his brother.

Galvanized into action, she turned, racing to Cormac's small cabin. After pounding on his door, she pushed it open when he didn't answer. Peering inside, her frantic motions froze as she saw a tidy home with no discernible personal touches. The bed was made, the stove cold to her touch, the coffee cup clean and hanging from a peg near the sink area. His clothes were gone, as was the keepsake rock he kept by the stove that Maura had given him this summer. Spinning, she ran to the livery.

"Mr. Harrison," she gasped out when she arrived. "Where's Cormac?"

He stared at her for a long assessing moment, causing a soft flush to rise on her cheeks. "Seems he had a desire to be elsewhere." He pointed over his shoulder with his thumb. "Left town this mornin' with Dunmore on Dunmore's last trip into the Territory before winter arrives. We won't be seein' him again until the snow thaws next spring. If ever."

"No," she gasped. "He wouldn't …" She swallowed what else she would say as she noticed the curious gleam in the liveryman's eyes and knew she had become the town's greatest source of gossip. "Thank you for informing me."

"Ma'am," he muttered, although the respect that used to tinge his voice was absent. He turned on his heel and ignored her, as he entered his tack room.

Niamh stumbled from the livery and held on to the doorway in a dazed stupor. After a moment, she forced her feet to move as she walked in the direction of her father's home. However, she came to an abrupt halt as Aileen's aunt, Janet Davies, waylaid her near the hotel.

"Ah, Mrs. Ahern, I have to admit I was delighted to hear the tale from Uriah of your downfall." She snickered as she beheld Niamh. Janet wore a fashionable dress in royal blue, the bright sheen faded after numerous washings. "It seems you are the black sheep of the O'Rourke family."

Niamh squared her shoulders and took a deep breath. Although it did little to calm her roiling emotions, she pasted on a serene smile, as she met Janet's mocking gaze. "I believe those who have fallen as low as you should know better than to throw stones." Her smile transformed into a genuine one as Janet stiffened with indignation. "I have family and friends who will help me. I do not have to rely on the dubious alliance with a transient man to whom loyalty and decency are unknown traits. Unlike you, I am not alone in this world."

Janet Davies reached out, gripping Niamh's forearm in a painful grip. "You'll come begging Uriah for his help. And I can't wait for the day he'll deny it to you. Your husband knew you were useless. Worthless." Her smile broadened with evil delight as she saw her words affected Niamh. "Now the town will too."

"No, the town will continue to learn you are a woman worth avoiding." She wrenched her arm free and stepped around Janet Davies.

"I find it fascinating his brother left too. Couldn't stand the thought of having to saddle himself with his brother's garbage, so he had to flee town." Janet cackled with glee as she saw Niamh stumble at her words before she walked away and turned for home.

After she arrived home, Niamh collapsed into a chair at the kitchen table. She heard the distant chortle of Maura as she played with Maggie, Aileen, and her mother; her younger brothers chattering; and the creak of a rocking chair. Although the kitchen was warm, with the stove always lit, she knew most of her family gathered in the living room, around the second stove her father had installed. She pushed herself to rise, to join them, but she found herself incapable.

The events of the morning continued to play through her mind.

Although Janet Davies's words had stung, they did not hurt her like Cormac's departure did. Why would he run away? She put her head on the table, as a sob burst forth.

"Niamh, love," Seamus murmured, as he entered the kitchen. After setting aside his tea mug, he wrapped an arm around her shoulder and sat beside her. "What's brought this on?"

"He left!" Niamh stammered out. "And I made him go. It's all my fault."

Rather than contradict her, Seamus held her close as she sobbed. "You hurt the lad. An' Dunmore was leavin' today. Cormac saw his chance an' took it." He sighed as Niamh sniffled. "You must have faith he'll come back to you, Niamh."

She shook her head, her shoulders stooped. "Why would he? I've given him no indication I want him." She closed her eyes, as tears coursed down her cheeks. "I've been so afraid ..."

When she remained quiet, Seamus sighed. "You'll find fear is a lonely bedfellow, my darling daughter."

Niamh stilled and turned to stare at her father, her gaze accusatory and filled with betrayal. "You knew he was leaving. You said, *he saw his chance and took it.*" At her father's nod, she scooted away from him, her head shaking repeatedly, as though dumbfounded at the disloyalty from someone she had always trusted. "How could you do that to me?"

With a gaze filled with patience and love, Seamus gripped her shoulders. "He wanted to ensure the lads would tend to his oxen. Your brothers don't have enough to do now that winter approaches, and the work will keep them out of trouble." He waited for Niamh to react, but she scrunched up her face and stared mutinously at his shoulder. "Think, Niamh. If his oxen are here, he'll return."

Niamh pushed away and rose, stumbling over her skirts and the chair, nearly tumbling into the stove. "No!" she cried, as she held a hand to her belly, as a deep, searing agony washed through her, more acute and more profound than anything she had ever felt with Connor. "No. I need him here. Now. And he left. And you let him go."

60

Seamus shook his head, his gaze filled with sadness. "*I* didn't, Niamh. *You* did. And 'tis that which you find so difficult to live with."

He rose, leaving her alone in the kitchen in her silent misery, as she contemplated a life without Cormac. A life she'd never had to imagine since the day she had met him.

~

After two miserable days, Cormac groaned as he emerged from the carriage in Virginia City. Although he could have chosen to spend the journey chatting with Dunmore, sitting on top of the stagecoach, Cormac had no desire for company or friendship. The handful of men who had made the journey scattered as soon as they had grabbed their bags. Rather than follow them, as they searched out places to stay or the varied entertainment offered in the burgeoning mining town, Cormac stared up and down the boardwalk, his satchel by his feet.

Dunmore ambled over after tying up his horses. "I'm headed to the livery and then to the café. I leave early tomorrow for Fort Benton. Want to make it back before the first storm hits."

Cormac scratched at his beard and shook his head. "I thought you'd spend the winter here. More to do here than in Fort Benton."

"Oh, I have my reasons for wanting to be there," Dunmore said cryptically. "If you come to your senses, you know where to find me."

Cormac watched the stagecoach driver walk away and then stared around at the small town. As they had first approached the town, it had felt like the stagecoach would fall off the face of the mountain as it dropped into the gully that held the growing mining town. Along the main street were the usual stores, bars, and cafés. In the distance, he could see openings to mines carved into the hills and sluices whittling away the dirt. Although not a large town, Cormac saw more people and much more commerce here than in Fort Benton.

He fought a desire to return to the familiar and forced himself to wander into a boarding house on the edge of town to rent a room. After a quick trip to the bathhouse and a hearty meal at a café, he wandered into one of the saloons. He had no desire for company of any kind, so he remained to one side of the long wooden bar, his shoulders hunched as he stooped over it. His alert gaze continually roved over the other patrons, alert to the activities of the men around him. However, none, except for the bartender, paid him any mind. Those present kept to themselves, commiserated with other miners about their inability to find the mother lode, or flirted with women in flashy dresses.

After swallowing another mouthful of rotgut, Cormac nodded goodbye to the barkeep and set out for his rented room at the boarding house. Although it would have been more economical to sleep on a cot in a shared room, he desired privacy after days spent in a stagecoach with relative strangers. As he walked toward the boarding house, he breathed in deeply of the woodsmoke-tinged air.

Unbidden, a memory invaded his thoughts.

"Why don't you like woodsmoke?" he teased, as he tossed another log into the stove and shut the grate. His brother, Connor, was out at the saloon and wouldn't learn of Cormac's return to town until the morning. Although Cormac had thought to leave the moment he had learned Connor wasn't home, Niamh had urged him inside to see how Maura had grown during the short time he'd been away.

"I never said I didn't like woodsmoke," she protested with a laugh, as she ladled out stew for their supper. "I simply don't like the work entailed in chopping, stacking, and hauling the wood."

Cormac froze with Maura suspended overhead, his gaze on Niamh, as Maura giggled with glee to kick her chubby legs in the air. "Are you telling me that Connor doesn't ensure you have enough wood? That you have to do that work?"

Niamh flushed and shrugged. "I do what I must."

After he had lowered Maura and sat with her on his lap, he shook his head. "You shouldn't have to do any of that work, Niamh. If Connor won't do it, I will."

"Cormac," Niamh said, with a warning shake of her head, "no. I shouldn't have said anything." She turned away to face the stove, her shoulders stooped,

as though with embarrassment about her relationship with her husband. "I will find a way."

He soundlessly rose and moved toward her with Maura in his arms. When he touched Niamh lightly on her shoulder, she jumped, spun around, and held up her arm, as though protecting herself. His eyes flared with shock and concern before a deep-seated rage settled inside his belly. "Shh, Niamh, I'd never hurt you." He paused a long moment, as he watched her pant and fight shame. "You're safe, Niamh. Maura's safe." He watched as his words eased her panic. and her breathing slowly calmed, although her embarrassment flared.

"I ... I don't know what came over me," she said, as she attempted a nonchalant shrug and smile. "I'm a bit jumpy tonight."

Cormac kissed Maura on her head as she became fussy with the undercurrent of emotions roiling between him and Niamh. "Are you certain that's all it is?"

"Yes," Niamh whispered, before clearing her throat and smiling a too-bright smile. "What else could it be?"

He nodded, gently patted her shoulder, and then sat again with Maura against his shoulder. "I don't want you worrying about chopping, hauling, and stacking wood, Niamh. If Connor doesn't do it, I will. It's the least I can do to make sure my niece doesn't freeze."

A pistol firing in the distance bolted him from his reverie, and he shook his head. "Damn fool," he muttered to himself. "Should have seen then what was as plain as day."

With a frustrated huff, he set off for his small room, unable to tamp down the emotions his memories wrought.

N iamh rocked a fussy Maura in the rocking chair, her throat parched after singing another lullaby. However, Maura seemed to calm with the sound of her mother's voice, so Niamh tried to continue to croon to her. Although her daughter was flushed and a little sweaty, it seemed like nothing more than a simple bout of teething. "My poor wee love," she whispered, as she kissed Maura's head. "Soon all your teeth will be in, and you'll have no more pain."

When she felt Maura go limp in her arms, she let out a sigh of relief and relaxed against the back of the chair. However, she knew she couldn't set Maura down, for, if she did, Maura would awaken and scream.

With a long sigh, Niamh let her eyelids drop, and a memory resurfaced.

Niamh stood, rocking a three-month-old Maura to and fro as she whimpered with colic. Nothing Niamh did calmed her, although she seemed a little more at ease when she was in her arms.

"Can't you quiet her down?" Connor demanded from a nearby chair. "All that whining and mewling is enough to make me wish we'd never had her."

"Connor!" Niamh gasped. "What a horrible thing to say." She gaped at her husband, holding her daughter even tighter in her arms, as though afraid Connor would snatch Maura from her and do her daughter bodily harm. "She's sufferin', and our job is to soothe her."

Connor rolled his eyes and kicked out his legs, as if to get comfortable. "Well, I'm in constant distress because my wife ignores me for that little whelp and never has energy for me anymore." His derisive gaze roved over Niamh, swaying side to side with his daughter. "She's been nothing but trouble since she was born."

Tears coursed down Niamh's cheeks. and Maura gave a small cry, as though sensing the strife between her parents. "Shh, little love, he doesn't mean it. He's had a bad day, is all. He'll love you like a father should."

Connor snorted. "If you believe I'll coddle that child the way the O'Rourkes coddled you, you're out of your mind. She'll receive a firm hand, as every woman should."

Niamh shivered and backed up a step. "She's a babe, Connor. She doesn't know better."

He stood and rolled his shoulders. "She'll learn." He looked around their barren house. "As there's nothing for me to do, and you're occupied, I'll be off." He barely spared her a backward glance before leaving.

When the door thudded after him, Niamh heaved out a sigh of relief, thankful for the relative peace of his absence. "Is this how it will always be?"

she whispered to herself, as she kissed the downy soft hair of her beloved daughter. "Me prayin' for his departure so I'll find peace?"

Maura gave a small yelp, and Niamh returned to the present. She kissed her daughter on her head again, as though linking the two memories. Belatedly she realized her cheeks were damp with her tears, and she pulled out a handkerchief to rub them dry.

"I'll always protect you, my darling," Niamh whispered, as she closed her eyes, her daughter held tight in her embrace.

CHAPTER 6

The following day, Niamh opened the back door to the insistent knocking, her harried flush paling at the sight of Sheriff Wilcox. "Sheriff," she whispered, as she stood in front of the door, blocking his entrance. Although she knew he could force his way in if he so desired, he was purported to be fair and calm. "Are you looking for my father?"

Leander Wilcox pushed at the large hat on his forehead, tipping it back, and his severe, penetrating gaze met her apprehensive one. Although he appeared pained to be on her father's back doorstep, he looked at her with a determination to fulfill his duty. "Please don't act coy, Mrs. Ahern. You know why I'm here."

She shivered at his serious tone and then nodded. In a whisper she said, "I do," and stepped aside so he could enter. She motioned for him to hang his coat on the rack near the stove and watched as he rubbed his hands together over the warmth of the stove. A shiver moved through him, as though he were warming up after a long time spent out-of-doors.

Niamh glanced to the kitchen's inner doorway, and she relaxed at the appearance of her father. He stood tall and proud, his gaze as foreboding as the sheriff's. "Da, Sheriff Wilcox is here to discuss the matter."

Seamus nodded and motioned for the sheriff to sit at the table. After pouring cups of tea, he sat beside Niamh, placing his large hand over hers in a sign of solidarity. "Sheriff, you might as well get on with whatever it is you believe you must say."

"Damn it, Seamus," Sheriff Wilcox muttered. "You know I hate being here and having to take the word of an interloper." He sighed, rubbing at his brown hair in his agitation. "However, too many townsfolk believe he is a lawyer, and Connor Ahern did. Enough to leave a written will with the man."

Seamus continued to stare at the sheriff, waiting in silence for him to say more. He made a small noise of discouragement when Niamh went to speak up, squeezing her hand to remain quiet.

"If that will is to be believed, Mr. Connor Ahern didn't want Mrs. Ahern raising their child. As the father, he had the right to determine his child's future. Unlike lawyers I knew when I lived in Arkansas, this Uriah Chaffee is only too willing to share the private documents of his clients with everyday citizens."

"Perhaps it is because his client is deceased," Niamh muttered.

"No," Seamus said. "His profession calls for more integrity than that." After a moment, he looked at the sheriff. "What are you suggesting?"

Sheriff Wilcox shrugged his shoulders and thumped a hand on the table. "I honestly don't know. I thought I'd seen just about everything, but this has confounded me. How can I, in good conscience, take a child, who's little more than a baby, away from her mother? And give her to a Madam?"

"Nora is a good woman," Seamus murmured, daring the sheriff to contradict him. He gave a terse nod when the sheriff held his peace rather than comment on the Madam.

"But she's not me," Niamh said.

"No," Seamus said. "Here is my proposal. I've discussed it with Mary, and she is in agreement. According to the will, the stipulation that Nora raise Maura is null and void once Niamh marries again."

Noting the shocked looked on the sheriff's face, Seamus's smile was filled with derision as he shook his head. "Chaffee forgot to inform you of that important detail, aye?"

"Aye," the sheriff muttered. "Makes me wonder what else Chaffee forgot to tell me."

"Thankfully Nora is loyal and cunning. We've seen the will, and we know what must be done. However, 'twill be a while before Niamh is ready to marry again. No matter what her feckless husband wrote in that will, Niamh was a loyal and honorable wife who needs time to mourn the death of her husband."

Sheriff Wilcox studied Niamh—who had bowed her head, as though moved by her father's words—and then Seamus, as though searching for sincerity. Wilcox nodded, indicating he would rather remain in the good graces of the O'Rourkes, the most influential family in Fort Benton, than align himself with the unknown Chaffee.

"In the meanwhile Nora will move in here with us. With my boys in Saint Louis, there is room for her. She will continue to run her establishment, but she will reside here, when she is not busy with her business."

Niamh gasped at her father's pronouncement, while the sheriff gaped at him, before bursting out laughing. "Only you, Seamus O'Rourke, could attempt to make such an arrangement sound respectable."

With a glower, Seamus glared at Leander. "Because it is." He waited until the sheriff sobered. "You, and everyone in this town, must be mad if you believe for one minute that I would allow my granddaughter to be separated from her mother."

Leander nodded, his gaze distant, as though deep in thought. After a few silent moments, a smile burst forth, and he fought a chuckle. "This complies with the demands of the will, in an irregular manner. However, I fear you haven't realized how the gossip will grow when the Madam moves in here."

Seamus leaned forward, as though to argue with the sheriff, only holding his tongue when Niamh squeezed his hand and shook her head.

"No, sir," Niamh said in a soft voice. "If you were a parent, you'd understand the only thing that matters is keeping my daughter with me. No matter the arrangement I must make or the gossip I must suffer. None of that matters, as long as I don't lose her."

The sheriff's eyes gleamed with respect as he looked at Niamh. "I understand better than you might believe." He rose. "I'll await word of the Madam's arrival here, and there will be no reason for me to visit again on this matter. If you have any need of my aid, please inform me."

Niamh remained seated as Seamus showed the sheriff to the door. After he had left, she stared at her father in shock. "Truly, Da, was there no other option?"

Her father studied her, one hip leaning against the doorjamb. "Have you thought of a better idea, love?"

Niamh shook her head. "Mum will suffer terribly with the Madam here. I can't believe she agreed to your proposal."

Seamus smiled tenderly at her, approaching her slowly, as she had been skittish of late. When she did not lean away from him, he cupped her jaw and looked deeply into her hazel eyes that reminded him of his beloved wife's eyes. "No, my darling daughter, this wasn't my idea. 'Twas your mother's. She wanted me to inform the sheriff it was mine, for she thought it would be less scandalous if such a scheme were to come from a man, but she proposed this."

"Why? She'll live under a cloud of speculation. That her husband now has wife and ..." Niamh broke off, as though embarrassed to say anything more.

"Aye, she knows what will be said." He waited a long moment before he murmured, "'Tis the measure of her love for you, Niamh, that she would suffer any disparaging remarks, any cruel judgments, to spare you the pain she suffered upon losing her children."

Niamh stared at him with wide-eyed disbelief, tears tracking down her cheeks. Her breaths were uneven and stuttered, as she tried to swallow a sob.

Nodding in understanding, Seamus kissed her forehead and left her alone in the kitchen to contemplate what was to come.

That evening, Niamh worked with Maggie to freshen up the bedroom Ardan, Kevin, and Declan had shared. The younger boys had removed two of the beds, storing them in the attic, and now the sisters were busy sweeping the floor, dusting the side tables and the bureau, and polishing the windows. Without the other beds crammed into the room, it was remarkably spacious, with space for a small writing desk added, and they had heard their father mutter something about finding a comfortable chair for the Madam.

Maggie whistled and sang as she worked, while Niamh remained in quiet contemplation. Finally Maggie broke off from a song she'd heard one of the steamboat crew sing the past summer, a racy tune she knew her father would disapprove of, and faced her sister. "What's the matter, Niamh?" she asked, as she pushed open the window to shake her dust rag outside to clean it, so she could start again. After she shut the window, she leaned on the windowsill. "I thought you'd be pleased the Madam is coming here."

Niamh rolled her eyes. "You even say the words *the Madam* as though she's some sort of exotic creature," Niamh muttered. "She's just a woman. A woman I fear is after Da. And will only cause trouble."

Maggie laughed. "You're much more foolish than I thought you'd be." When Niamh stood with her hands fisted on her hips, Maggie shrugged. "I always thought an older sister would be wise, giving me sound advice. Instead you seem muddled."

"And how are you so wise?" Niamh asked with a defiant tilt of her jaw. She looked her younger sister over from head to foot and snorted derisively. "You've barely lived."

Maggie tapped the rag against her leg and smiled. "I'm a good observer, and, although I know what fear is, I refuse to allow it to rule me."

"Said like a child," Niamh snapped, as she spun away to polish the bureau.

Maggie snapped her fingers together, as though finally figuring out a riddle. "That's it, isn't it? I don't know the full extent of your fear because I don't have a child." She paused as she watched her sister, still in her manic swiping of the bureau.

"Pray you never do," Niamh rasped.

"Have a child or know the fear you do?" Maggie asked in a low voice.

Niamh spun to stare at her, her expression a mixture of antipathy and weariness. "The fear," she said in a defeated voice. "I'd never wish to not have Maura. She's the best part of me."

"That's not true, Niamh," Maggie said, gently stroking a hand down her sister's back, ignoring Niamh's instinctual stiffening. "Maura is wonderful and loving and trusting. All things I believe you must have been at one time. For how else could you have been?" When Niamh turned to stare at her sister with abject befuddlement, Maggie shrugged. "You never would have married a man like your husband if you hadn't been like Maura."

Niamh closed her eyes and fisted a hand on top of the bureau. "I never want anything to befall my girl, but I dread her ever being as naive, as stupid, as I was."

Maggie squeezed her arm and shook her head. "She won't be, Niamh, for, unlike you, she has you." Maggie bit her lip. "And, if she's very lucky, and her mother isn't a fool, she'll have a man who loves her as much as a father to raise her. And to protect her."

Niamh nodded, turning back to polish. When her mother's frantic voice rang out from downstairs, calling for Niamh, her polishing rag dropped to the floor. Niamh raced from the room, with Maggie on her heels.

"Mum?" Niamh asked, panting and red-faced, her gaze filled with panic as she saw her mother sitting in a rocking chair with Maura in her arms.

Mary met Niamh's gaze, unable to hide the terror in hers and reached out a hand to her daughter. "I just picked her up," she whispered. "I thought she'd slept too long and wanted time with my granddaughter." She fought a sob. "She's burnin' up, Niamh. An' havin' trouble breathin.'" A tear leaked down Mary's cheek and dripped onto Maura's head as she continued to hold her granddaughter.

"No!" Niamh screamed, reaching for her daughter. Her hands roved over her, frantic and shaking, as her soft touch confirmed the truth of her mother's words. "No," she cried, as she fought tears. "We will see her through this, Mum. We have to."

Mary nodded, rocking Maura in her arms, as she crooned a soft lullaby to her.

Maggie moved to Niamh, wrapping an arm around her sister's shoulder and pulling her close. "We'll find a way to lower her fever and to keep her healthy, Niamh."

"No doctor's in town," Niamh said dumbly. "He left with Dunmore and Cormac. Wanted to be in a place during winter where he'd have more patients." She swayed in place before falling to her knees. "What will we do with no doctor?"

Maggie smiled. "He isn't the only one with knowledge." Her smile froze when she looked to the living room doorway. "Oh, hello," she said with an impersonal smile. She glanced at her mother and sister, who were preoccupied with her niece, and moved in Madam Nora's direction. "You've arrived in the midst of our little crisis."

Nora stood in the hallway with a small bag at her feet. "I'm sorry to interrupt, but I had thought I'd be expected. No one answered my knock at the back door, and I had no desire to again be ignored at the front door."

Maggie gave a half shrug of resignation. "You'll be living here, so you should feel free to come and go as you please." She flushed. "I'm afraid Niamh and I didn't completely finish cleaning your room. It's almost ready." She stilled when the Madam placed a soft hold on her forearm and nodded to the scene of Mary and Niamh with Maura. "Maura's ill," Maggie whispered, answering the unspoken question. "We must find a way to heal her."

Madam Nora nodded. "Never fear. Where there is knowledge, and a will, there is a way. I have books, plenty of them, in my office. After I'm settled, you and I will return to determine what we need."

Maggie smiled delightedly and, with an added spring in her step, motioned for the Madam to follow her.

~

Niamh sat in the room she shared with Maura on the first floor, watching as Maura slept. She prayed for Maura's fever to break, for the deep cough to resolve, and for her baby to be the free-spirited girl racing around her parents' house once again. Yearning for Cormac's strong arms to wrap around her, reassuring her that everything would be fine, Niamh pulled her shawl tighter around her shoulders.

Although she attempted to ignore her sorrow at Cormac's absence, she was unable to deny her need to have him here with her now. He had always comforted her when he was in town, and the knowledge that he would return had encouraged her to continue to smile and to find moments of joy in each day. Now she feared he would never return to her. That she had ruined her chance with him. Due to her fear and her cowardice. She sighed as she rubbed her head and stared at her sick daughter. "What if I'm never brave enough for him?" she whispered aloud, before giving voice to her greatest fear. "What if I lose them both?"

She shivered, uncertain she would survive such loss. With a strength of will borne of desperation and self-preservation, she forced herself to think of something else. The faint light, her unimaginable exhaustion, and the late hour reminded her of the first days and months after the birth of Maura. Niamh hadn't known what she was doing, and, without her mother or an aunt to guide her, she had stumbled and had to find her way on her own. Her gaze was unfocused as she stared at a candle flame, a memory from that time returning to her.

She barely had the energy to push her foot to rock the chair, but she managed to keep the chair in motion, both to comfort herself and her daughter, barely one month old. Niamh breathed deeply, inhaling the sweetest scent imaginable. A scent that she knew would keep her enthralled and would ensure her daughter's protection forever. With bleary-eyed wonder, she gazed at the perfection of her baby. Chubby cheeks, silky soft to the touch and pearly white. A downy soft head of hair that made Niamh want to rub a gentle hand over it or give it a kiss. Ten perfect little toes and ten perfect little fingers to squeeze and to marvel at. How had such a beautiful being come from her?

Niamh chuckled, her finger caressing one of Maura's cheeks. Then Maura opened her mouth, making a pop *noise as she finished breastfeeding. "Are you done then, you wee glutton?" Niamh teased, with a kiss to her daughter's head, as she did up the front of her dress. "Come. Let me change you, and then we can both sleep a few hours."*

"Stop your caterwauling," Connor bellowed. "Don't you know some of us like to sleep when it's dark?"

Niamh made a soothing noise as Maura's eyes widened with alarm at the loud, abrading noise. However, with Niamh's comfort, Maura settled again. Soon Niamh had her in a small bassinette, which her da had had a local man make for her.

With a satisfied groan, Niamh crawled back into bed, hopeful for an hour or two of sleep before she had to rise again. However, Connor was awake, agitated, and eager for an argument. She rolled onto her side, her back to him, hopeful he would calm and would allow her to rest.

"You think rolling away from me, ignoring your husband, is going to make me forget all the duties you are shirking because you are spoiling that brat?"

She gasped, rolling onto her back to stare at him with wide-eyed shock. "Brat? She's barely a month old. How can you say such a thing?"

He leaned on one elbow and glared down at her. "She takes up all your time, energy, and focus. You have nothing left for me or our home. Tonight, there wasn't even dinner ready when I was hungry."

"For the love of God, Connor, I just had a baby. One month ago. You know my father said you could eat with them any time you needed to."

"Like I'd want to be surrounded by O'Rourkes," he hissed. "And watch them turn their noses up at me because they are more successful than I am?" He shook his head. "No. I refuse to be their nightly entertainment."

"That's not how it would be," she coaxed. "They'd get to know you better. And perhaps you could start working at the warehouse or the store."

"I work! I earn money at the gambling tables!" he snapped. "I have no need of their charity." His eyes flashed with anger, and his cheeks were flushed. "You think you're cunning, but you aren't, Niamh." At the flash of uncertainty in her gaze, he smiled with satisfaction. "You will cease shirking your duties. You will focus your attentions on me, rather than that mewling excuse for a baby."

"Please, Connor, she's ours. She's beautiful and precious."

He leaned over her, his gaze darkened with loathing. "No, she's worthless. Because you gave me a daughter. A daughter, Niamh!" His breath came out in agitated pants. "How could you humiliate me like that? You know that a man, like me, always deserved sons. Not a worthless daughter."

"Daughters aren't worthless," Niamh said in a quavering voice, her eyes filled with tears she fought to keep from shedding.

"Of course they are. They grow up to be women, who are only a burden and are only good for two things. Pleasing a man and giving him sons." He stared at her derisively. "You've failed in the two things you were meant to do." He flopped onto his back with a sigh of disgust. "And I'm stuck with you for the rest of my life. I can't believe fate has been so cruel to me."

Niamh rolled onto her side, curling into herself, as though to find a way to protect herself from his harsh words. However, she had no armor that could prevent his words from piercing her dreams and the softest, gentlest part of her. When she heard him begin to snore, she gave in to her tears, sobbing into her pillow.

Niamh jolted when the door opened, her gaze darting to the woman standing in the doorway. "Madam," she rasped. "I never thought to see you here."

"Why wouldn't I be?" the Madam asked, an amused glint in her gaze. "I live here now. Well, at least until you have the sense to marry again. And I work odd hours at the Bordello."

Niamh glanced outside, but the dawn's rays seemed hours away. "I would think you'd be needed there at this hour."

Nora waved away Niamh's concern. "It's a quiet night. Most of my girls ended up spending the evening playing cards with each other, rather than entertaining any men. I fear they'll spend too many evenings like this as winter settles in." She smiled wryly. "I tell them to enjoy such times, for they'll be busy again come spring with the arrival of the steamboats."

Niamh stared at her with fascination. "Don't you have any remorse for the life you are allowing those women to lead?" She shivered as though at the thought.

Nora shrugged and sat on one of the wooden chairs near Niamh, her intelligent gaze roving over a sleeping Maura. "Very little. I have never coerced a woman into this life. And I know that all of them would have suffered a fate far worse than the one they are currently living, had they not joined me at the Bordello." She nodded as Niamh gaped at her. "Alone, starving, perhaps even murdered. I provide them with food, shelter, and protection. Ezra is a good man and will never allow anyone to harm them."

Niamh frowned and shook her head. "It still seems ... like a horrible choice," she whispered.

"Not all have family, Niamh," Nora said in a gentle voice filled with soft rapprochement. "Few are fortunate enough to have a father like Seamus."

Niamh nodded and closed her eyes.

"And even fewer have a mother like Mary."

She stiffened at Nora's words. "You barely know her," Niamh rasped. "How can you say such a thing?"

Nora tapped Niamh on her arm and murmured, "I've never met a mother willing to have a Madam move into her home to protect her daughter and granddaughter. Mary expressed no concern for herself or her reputation. She has so much faith in her husband that she is not threatened by me. And she has the strength of character to stand up to any and all censure that will come her way by small-minded towns-folk. All because she loves her daughter."

Nora paused as she saw Niamh consider her words. "I've met few, in all my travels, fortunate enough to have a Seamus in their lives, never mind a Mary. You are doubly blessed." She rose. "I will continue to pray your daughter returns to good health."

Niamh sat in stunned silence, as she watched the Madam slip from the room.

～

Three days after his arrival in Virginia City, Cormac wandered up and down the boardwalk of his new town, marveling at the town carved into the narrow gulch. Although he knew he should feel at home, as one frontier town was little different from another, he felt a wave a longing for his home in Fort Benton. For the people he had left behind. For those who considered him family.

He wished he had had the sense to return to Fort Benton with Dunmore. Now that Cormac was stuck here until spring, all he yearned for was to be there. To see the cliffs gleaming in the late-afternoon sun. To watch the mighty Missouri change with the seasons. To see Niamh again, and, if there was any mercy in this world, to hold her in his arms once more.

Although he knew Niamh had memories and fears to overcome, he realized he wanted to be the one to help her conquer them. He paused and closed his eyes, as he let out a deep breath. "Please want me to be the one," he whispered. "I couldn't bear for you to find another man, anyone other than me." He ducked his head and slammed his hand against a nearby wall at the futility of his situation.

"Cormac?" called out a distantly familiar voice. "Why are you attacking my wall?"

Cormac's head jerked up at the sound of his name, and he stared with bleary eyes for a moment at a familiar man. "Buford? What are you doing here? I thought you went to Helena." He shook his head in confusion at seeing Buford Hunt in Virginia City. His paunch was larger and his hair thinner, although his smile appeared more genuine as he stared at Cormac.

"I own this café. I took what I earned from selling my business in Fort Benton and purchased this one. Much more profitable to run an establishment in a town that has commerce more than only a few months a year."

Cormac fought a smile. "Hopefully you have as good a cook as Deirdre."

Buford made a grunt of disgust and then spoke in a low voice, in case someone was listening in. "I doubt I'll ever find a cook as good as Deirdre. But my cook is good, and the customers come back again, even though more options are available in this town."

"Well, congratulations, Buford." Cormac pushed away from the café. "I ate somewhere else last night." He waved at a forgettable place a little ways down the boardwalk. "If your food is better, you don't have much competition."

Clapping Cormac on the back, Buford urged him inside. "Come in. Tell me all the news about Fort Benton. Although I'm enjoying my life here, I do miss everyone there." He fought a chagrined smile. "Even the meddling O'Rourkes."

After he had sat and wrapped his hands around the coffee mug to warm them up, Cormac speared Buford with a warning look. "You know better than to speak against the O'Rourkes with me."

"Well, I wasn't so sure. Seein' as you're here, and they're there. Thought you might have had a falling out finally with your brother or one of them."

Cormac paled and shook his head, as any levity seeped away at the mention of his brother. "You didn't hear," he murmured. "Connor died. A few weeks ago." He cleared his throat and shook his head again, as though to dispel the reality of his brother's death.

Buford sat with a *thud* at a chair across from him. "Oh, now, son, I'm sorry. I never took to him, but I would never have wished him ill." After a moment, his gaze turned calculating. "How's his widow?"

Cormac sent a warning glare at Buford, earning a grunt of satisfaction from the older man. "Mourning," Cormac said, hissing as he burned his tongue on a sip of the too-hot coffee.

"I'd think a smart man would remain in town to offer a shoulder as it's needed."

"Buford," Cormac said, unable to hide a small smile at the man's incorrigible comment. "If Dunmore hadn't already left for Fort

Benton, I'd be on my way with him. I've realized Fort Benton's home, and I miss it."

Buford stared at him with confusion. "Dunmore hasn't left yet. He plans to depart tomorrow. I'm certain you can find him at the livery."

Cormac froze at the news, staring slack-jawed at Buford, as the café owner nodded at him to reassure he wasn't lying. After a moment, Cormac rose and squeezed Buford on the shoulder, before spinning to race to the livery. Upon his entry into the darkened interior, he paused to allow his eyes to adjust. "Dunmore?" he called out.

After a moment, Dunmore poked his head out of a room toward the back of the livery. "I thought you'd never come to your senses."

"And I thought you were more worried about the weather."

Dunmore ambled toward him and shrugged. His lanky frame belied a steely strength, while his relaxed appearance hid his cautious nature. Dunmore's blue-green eyes glinted with frustration as he stared at Cormac. "I was eager to find someone, but he evaded me again." He kicked at a dried piece of horse dung, launching it against a stall door.

Cormac studied him a long moment and then whispered, "Jacques Bergeron." At Dunmore's nod, Cormac sighed. "Maggie thinks of you as a brother."

"Perhaps, but she's young yet and just turned eighteen. And I'm not so decrepit I can't wait a few years for her to discover I'm more than a sibling." No bitterness laced his tone, nor did he appear impatient with his current predicament. "However, I promised Seamus I'd keep an ear out for the man's whereabouts, and I know Bergeron's had a patch of luck. He won't return with me this trip, as I expect to have only one passenger, but I fear he'll return next season."

Cormac took a step toward Dunmore. "I'm your passenger."

"Of course you are, unless you truly are an *eejit*, as the O'Rourkes would call you." He clapped Cormac on the shoulder. "I'm to the bathhouse. We leave tomorrow at dawn."

Cormac nodded, watching Dunmore leave, a sense of peace filling Cormac that he would be in Fort Benton by week's end.

CHAPTER 7

M ary walked the short distance to the café, opting to take the long route there and to walk by the river. She relished every moment she spent with her family but also needed a few moments to herself each day. Pausing to stare at the muddy river water, she said a silent prayer that Maura would improve and that Niamh would find the happiness that had always eluded her. Although Mary worried about her three sons, who were so far away in Saint Louis for the winter, she tried not to focus her concern on them. As Seamus coaxed her during their quiet time together at night, she needed to have faith in their judgment and good sense. She refused to believe they would not return to her, for she could not imagine their family remaining apart for longer than this one winter season.

"I'm surprised the townsfolk allow you to walk among them," Janet Davies called out as she approached Mary.

Mary sighed and closed her eyes for a fleeting moment, any peace in her silent musings destroyed by the arrival of Aileen's contemptuous aunt. Mary turned to meet the challenging stare of a woman who did not understand the meaning of the words *family* or *loyalty* or *shame*. "'Twould think it would be you who would cower in fear, not me," Mary replied with a wry smile.

Janet huffed out a breath, her bosom straining the silver buttons of her evergreen-colored wool coat. "I have never done a thing in my life to warrant such censure."

"No, … other than attempting to force your beloved niece into a loveless marriage. Oh, an' stealin' the money sent home for her from her father for almost two decades. An' lyin' about never havin' heard from her father. An' spinnin' malicious lies to Aileen about her lack of beauty an' intelligence. An' blaming a helpless child for your loveless spinster life." Mary raised an eyebrow as she watched her adversary in an assessing manner as she ticked off Janet Davies's offenses. "Should I continue?"

Janet stroked a hand down the fine wool of her coat, which, by all appearances, looked new. "I've never harbored a brothel owner in my house."

Mary beamed at her. "'Twould be an edifyin' experience for you." She laughed at Janet's horrified expression. "She's a remarkable woman who exemplifies every characteristic you lack."

Scoffing and rolling her eyes, Janet rested a hand on her hip. "I'm certain she does. If knowing how to entice a worthless man to my bed is the skill I need to master, I will forever be a novice."

Watching Janet with a sly expression, Mary smiled. "But he wasn't worthless, was he? An' your sister won him, much to your chagrin." When Janet's face puckered up, as though she'd just sucked on a lime, Mary nodded. "You would have done well to learn a little from both your sister and a woman like Nora." After a long pause, Mary said in a soft voice, "What separates Nora from a woman like you, Janet, is that Nora understands loyalty. To family. To friends." Any levity had faded as Mary stared at the woman who had attempted to ruin Kevin's happiness. "Nora understands what is sacred and will never threaten those bonds."

Janet sneered at her. "Little is sacred in this life. That's something you and your family have yet to learn."

Mary shared a long look with Janet. "So you may believe right now, especially as you have aligned yourself with a man such as Mr. Chaffee." She paused. "Do you assume we'll forget your association with such a man because of your relation to Aileen?" Mary shook her head. "We'll never forget what you've encouraged him to do."

Flushing beet red, Janet fisted her hands at her sides as she leaned toward Mary. "You don't know what it is to survive solely by your wits. You've always had everything handed to you." She smiled as Mary stared at her with astonishment. "And he did nothing except uphold his duty to the law."

Raising her brows, Mary asked, "Omitting essential aspects of Connor's wishes was how he was taught to fulfill his obligation to his profession?" She shook her head. "An' you're a fool to believe a man like Uriah will ever support you as your family could have. You've sacrificed loyalty for the false promises of a man who will only ever show dedication to himself. After all, he remained here this winter because he had to flee Virginia City or suffer for his sins. 'Tis our misfortune he missed the last boat south. He's a man who will only ever be faithful to himself, and God help the woman who doesn't understand that about him." Mary leaned forward and said in a low voice, "Something I have far too much knowledge of." She straightened and ran a hand over her practical navy wool skirt. "Now, if you'll excuse me, I'm expected at the café."

Without a backward glance, she turned toward the café, leaving Janet Davies sputtering in indignation.

Niamh stumbled from her bed to Maura's, after awaking with a start from her nap. She fell into a chair by her daughter's bedside, her hands instinctively reaching forward to run over her daughter. Sighing with frustration, she felt the heat emanating from her daughter's forehead, signaling her fever had yet to break. "Maura, oh, my little love," she whispered, as a tear tracked down her cheek. "Please fight."

Niamh stiffened and then relaxed as her sister, Maggie, wrapped an arm around her and leaned against her side. Although Maggie had been sitting in the other bedside chair, Niamh had ignored her. "She still has the fever, but it's not as high, and her breathing has calmed. She will recover."

"How can you say that? You're not a healer," Niamh snapped and then flushed, her cheeks as rosy as her ailing daughter's. "I'm sorry."

Maggie shrugged. "I might not have been trained, but I've had to learn a lot while living out in the wilds with my family. And I enjoy it. Besides, Madam Nora has many interesting books, and it's been a pleasure reading some of them these past few days." She pulled her sister close, ignoring Niamh's prickliness. "Come. You know you can lean on me. On Mum. You have to learn that you aren't alone in your struggles."

Niamh tugged a cloth from her pocket to swipe at her nose, although she did relax into her sister's embrace. "I have been, for so long."

Maggie made a soothing noise and kissed Niamh on her head, acting like the elder sister. "Your husband was a scoundrel, but it doesn't mean it was your fault, Niamh. I don't understand why you hold yourself apart from us or why you'd push Cormac away. He's a good man."

Niamh made a derisive noise. "You do the same thing with any man who shows you interest."

Easing away from Niamh, Maggie flushed and then studied Niamh. "Then we both have memories we must banish." With an impish smile, Maggie said, "Besides, I'm young yet. I don't want to marry when I've just turned eighteen."

The rosy flush faded as Niamh gaped at her sister. "Your birthday! Your first birthday with us, and we didn't celebrate. Because of me."

Maggie lifted a shoulder. "I'll hopefully have another here. And it didn't seem right to have a party while the threat of the Madam taking Maura away loomed. And then Cormac departed, and now Maura's sick." Maggie ran a hand over the blankets covering her niece, her astute gaze taking in Maura's calm breathing as she slept. "Although, if you wanted to bake me a cake when Maura's feeling better, I'd never complain."

"Oh, if you aren't an O'Rourke!" Niamh said with a giggle. She immediately covered her mouth, her eyes wide and filled with embarrassment, as she glanced at her daughter sleeping peacefully. "I shouldn't …" She shook her head.

"What, Niamh?" Maggie whispered. "Feel joy? Laugh? Smile?" She paused as Niamh ducked her head. "Are those a few of the things he tried to beat out of you?" When Niamh's head jerked up, her gaze filled with astonishment and humiliation, Maggie nodded. "There is never any shame in overcoming cruelty, Niamh. And never shame in finding happiness again."

Maggie moved to stand, but Niamh clasped her arm. "How are you this wise?"

"I speak with Mum. She reassures me."

"Mum," Niamh gasped, the word laced with longing and pain. "I'm the reason she left." At Maggie's confused look, Niamh motioned to Maura. "I was sick, like Maura. But I had typhus. And I was so much work." Niamh ducked her head. "She was pregnant with you and already tired. I can't imagine she relished caring for me, when all she wanted was to rest and to prepare for you."

Maggie sat in perplexed silence for a few moments, as she watched her niece. "You believe Mum left Da, our brothers, and you because she didn't want the burden of caring for a sick child?"

Niamh nodded. "We were told she died soon afterward. I always knew I had been the one to kill her. And then, when she came back, I knew I was the reason she hadn't wanted to be with us."

Maggie sighed and shook her head. "You never would win a logic contest, sister." When Niamh bit her lip at an unexpected burst of laughter, Maggie smiled. "You've heard the story. You know why Mum and Da were separated. A nun put Mum and me in a small shack to keep us safe from the typhus, while another told Da that we'd died and had already been buried. It was all a horrible misunderstanding, and it had nothing to do with you." Maggie emphasized the last sentence.

When Niamh looked unconvinced, Maggie said, "If what you say is true, then Mum should have found a way to abandon me when I had measles. I wouldn't have been worth the work or the worry. But she didn't. She cared for me and loved me through it. As she did you, Niamh. That's who Mum is."

Niamh stared at her with dawning wonder. "You were ill, Maggie?"

"Of course I was. No child is never ill, Niamh. Not in our world." She rose, squeezing her sister's shoulder. "Let go of your mistaken guilt, Niamh. It isn't fair to you or to Mum."

~

That evening, while her da watched over a resting Maura, Niamh slipped into the kitchen. She paused as she heard her mother singing in her sweet, pure voice. It was an old song, a song Mary had sung frequently when Niamh was a child. Memories washed over her —of her rushing forward, hugging her mother and receiving a kiss on her head, as her mother enfolded her in a warm embrace. Of being held close when she needed a few moments of reassurance. Of feeling cherished and adored. Always her mum expressed her joy at Niamh's presence. Her mum never hid her pride in her smart, beautiful daughter. Never was Niamh made to feel a burden by her mother.

Tears coursed down her cheeks as she stared at her mum. "You always wanted us. Wanted *me*," she whispered.

Somehow Mary heard her and spun to stare at her, her hazel eyes gleaming with a mixture of hope and fear. "Always." She lifted her arms, as though to welcome Niamh close, as she had so many times before when Niamh was a wee girl. Yet, when Niamh remained across the room from her mum, Mary's arms dropped to her sides, her gaze showing her disappointment.

Niamh's breath came fast and shallow, and she fell to her knees, as a low keening wail emerged. She covered her face with her palms, stifling any outward signs of emotion, but she continued to rock to and fro as she knelt on the floor.

"Niamh, love, is it Maura?" When Niamh shook her head, Mary knelt in front of her, her gentle hands caressing Niamh's shoulders and head. "You are safe and loved here, my beloved daughter."

"Why did you have to go away?" Niamh stammered out, as she

clutched at her belly, her head on her knees as her shoulders shook. "I *nee-eeded* you so much."

Wrapping her daughter in her arms, Mary rocked her in place. "As I needed you, my beautiful daughter. I dreamed of you every night. Prayed you would grow to be the kind, wonderful woman you are."

Niamh shuddered and pushed out of her mother's arms, meeting her mum's kind, loving gaze. "But I'm not good. I'm not considerate." She dropped her gaze, so she wouldn't have to admit her worst faults to her mother. "I'm mean and jealous and spiteful."

Mary urged Niamh to sit up, and she gripped her daughter's shoulders. She stared deeply into eyes that matched hers in color, beauty, and depth of emotion. "Never have you been those things, nor will you be." She paused as she saw doubt in Niamh's gaze. "I can only imagine what you suffered with Connor, but his truths are not yours, Niamh."

Niamh bit her lip before whispering, "But I wished him dead. And then he died. It's my fault he died."

With a smile filled with tenderness and love, Mary shook her head. "You didn't cause him to act as he did. You didn't cause him to threaten another's safety." Mary paused, taking a deep breath. "Do you believe I am a good woman, worthy of your father's esteem? Of his devotion and love?"

Niamh stared with wide-eyed wonder at her mother. "Yes," she breathed. "You never faltered. Never, in your love for us or for Da." She closed her eyes. "I was bitter and jealous when you returned." She ducked her head. "I'm sorry."

"No, Niamh, love, that's not my point." She waited for Niamh to meet her gaze again. "I prayed, every night, for my second husband to die. For him to leave me and my children in peace." She smiled with tender understanding as Niamh watched her with astonishment. "Does that make me a horrible woman? Does that make me a woman undeserving of love, friendship, or esteem?"

"No," Niamh whispered. "But you don't understand, Mum. I ... I did something awful."

Mary cupped her daughter's cheek and watched her with gentle loyalty. "Loving another while married to a man who never inspired devotion does not make you horrible. 'Tis not awful. For I continued to love Seamus and all my beautiful children while married to Francois." She nodded, as Niamh's eyes widened with shock at her mother's blunt words. "'Tis a pity you chose the wrong brother."

Niamh lurched forward, burying her face in her mother's shoulder as she sobbed. "I missed you, Mum. I missed you so much. I wish I'd had your wise counsel. Things might have been so different."

"*Shh*, my darling girl. God willing, you will have a second chance with the man of your heart." She paused as Niamh blubbered into her shoulder. She whispered, "What matters is we are reunited. And we'll never be separated again." She kissed her daughter's head, holding her close and rocking her, as Niamh sought solace from her mum as she had when she was a girl.

~

M ary sat on her bed, her gaze distant, as silent tears coursed down her cheeks. Although the room was cool, she sat in only her flannel nightgown, her graying auburn hair unbound and flowing down her back. She envisioned Niamh in her cradle, her downy soft hair aglow in the gentle fire's light, as she kicked her feet up and gurgled at her. Niamh as she stumbled and chased after her older brothers, determined not to be left behind. Kissing her palm as Niamh cried after scraping it open when falling from a rock wall.

The door opened to the small bedroom she shared with Seamus, but she remained lost to her memories. When Seamus's arms wrapped around her, she relaxed at the feel of his gentle touch and his distinctive smell.

"*A ghrá*," he whispered. "Are you well, my love?"

"Oh, Shay," she whispered, as she pressed her face into his neck. "Niamh wanted my comfort this evening. 'Tis the first time since Montreal that I've been able to console her."

He made a soothing sound and continued to hold her.

"Do you know what it's like to finally hold my wee Niamh in my arms? To know she wanted me to soothe her?" Mary wrapped her arms around her husband as a sob burst forth. "'Tis as though she finally trusts me."

"For some of our children, 'twill take them longer to understand you aren't leaving again. That you will always be here when they need you."

She backed away and stared at him with confusion. "I know I wasn't here, Shay. I know I have no right to doubt or to question what occurred during my absence." She dropped her gaze but then firmed her shoulders and stared at him with a hint of disappointment. "How could you have given your blessing for her to marry such a man?"

"Mary," Seamus murmured, a hint of reproach in his voice. "You don't know what it was like."

"Help me to understand," she pleaded. "I need to know why Niamh had to suffer so. Why she continues to suffer now." She swiped at her cheeks. "'Tis unfair."

"Aye, 'tis." He paused, closing his eyes. "None of us acknowledged how much we suffered at the loss of you. We acted as though we had recovered from losing the one person who made our house a home. Who made us a family." His jaw tensed. "Colleen had died, and the younger lads needed comfort as they mourned their mum. I ... I didn't focus on Niamh as I should have. I didn't realize her loss of a mother was different than the loss the boys had suffered."

"Seamus," Mary whispered.

"She needed your wise counsel as she turned from girl to woman. She needed your advice and humor as she first noticed boys." He half smiled. "She didn't need overbearing brothers and an overprotective father, who wanted her to stay as far away as possible from any lad who might pay her attention. Who might call on her and attempt to turn her head with pretty, but meaningless words." His eyes glowed with torment. "I never allowed her to go walking with a lad. For how could any man be good enough for *mo leanbhán,* my baby."

"Oh, *a chuisle,* you can't blame yourself. You did all you could do for her and the boys." She rubbed her nose over his neck and sighed. "We have to accept she made a horrible decision in marrying Connor."

His hold on her tightened, as he pulled her even closer. "Aye, an' pray she has the sense to pick a better man the next time she marries."

Mary breathed into his ear. "'Tisn't a matter of picking the man. 'Tis a matter of her believing she deserves him."

"Feck," Seamus muttered before apologizing. "Why did I think 'twould be easier to be their father as they grew? I thought the problems facin' them would diminish."

Mary laughed softly. "No, my love." She kissed his neck. "My heartbeat," she murmured, in English this time, rather than in Irish, the term he had taught her that he loved to hear. "No, their problems are much more complicated as they grow and are not as easily solved with a hug and a kiss."

"Ah, that's where you are wrong. For I know you eased an ache in Niamh's heart that she's carried for eighteen years tonight with your love." He kissed her below her ear. "With your kiss." His arms tightened again around her. "With your hug." He sighed with contentment to hold her close. "For, if there's one thing I know, *a ghrá mo chroí,* everything is better with your love." He felt her shiver at calling her the love of his heart in Irish.

She pushed back, cupping his face in her hands, as her thumbs slid over his cheeks. "These months since I've returned have been as a dream to me."

"Ah, lass, for me too." A quiet joy lit his cobalt-blue eyes as he gazed at her. "The best part, my Mary, is that we never have to awaken. This is how our life will be for all time."

She sighed with pleasure, resting her head on his chest, as he kissed the top of it.

CHAPTER 8

Three days later, Maura improved with the speed and impatience of children. She was already out of bed, playing with her aunts, uncles, and grandparents. Although Niamh worried Maura would sicken again with too much activity, Maura seemed to know when she needed to rest. She would find someone's lap, curl up, and be asleep within moments. Every time Maura chose someone other than her mother, Niamh had to fight an instinctual jealousy.

This morning, Maura had curled onto the Madam's lap, as the Madam had found a quiet seat in the living room in the sun. Although Niamh had believed the sight of her daughter nestled on the Madam's lap would be incongruous; in reality, it was touching.

Madam Nora stroked a manicured hand over Maura's back and kissed her reddish curls as she murmured soft words to her as she slept. Her expression held a yearning for many more moments like this.

Niamh stood as a silent sentry to Nora's secret longing, as a tear tracked down Nora's cheek. Finally she whispered, "I'm glad you have this time with her."

Nora smiled, although it wasn't the practiced smile of a Bordello owner. It was a resigned smile of a woman who had had to give up her heart's desire. "I never thought to have such a moment with your daughter. She's rather free with her love."

Stepping into the living room, Niamh sighed. "I'm thankful she doesn't remember what life with her father was like. She remains trusting and loving."

Shaking her head, Nora's eyes gleamed with challenge. "You'll never accept the truth, will you?"

Stiffening at the perceived criticism, Niamh clasped her hands in front of her. "I'm afraid I don't understand."

Nora reached forward and gripped one of Niamh's fisted hands. "Maura isn't affectionate and trusting because she doesn't remember. She's the way she is because she never had to doubt your love. Nor your family's love. Your constancy has given her security, Niamh."

Tears poured from Niamh's eyes, until they dripped off her chin. "I didn't know what to do, Madam." She flushed at the admission and ducked her head.

"Few do in your situation. I remain thankful it didn't become so dire you were compelled to kill him." Nora paused. "Or his brother was so driven. For I'd hate for you to lose your chance for happiness."

Niamh shrugged and stared out the window a moment. "I doubt he'll return until next year."

Nora squeezed her hand again. "Be ready when he does. For a man like Cormac Ahern needs to know his woman, the woman he loves, missed him." She paused and looked down at Maura in her arms.

Ignoring her discomfort to have such a conversation with the Madam, Niamh stared at her with wide-eyed fascination. "What else should I do? Should I know?"

Nora's lips turned up, as though amused at being considered an oracle as to the ways of men. "He's a man, Niamh. He needs affection, and he needs to be able to show you his affection." Her gaze sobered, as she saw Niamh shiver at the thought. "He needs to know you'll love him, Niamh. As he loves you."

"How do you know he cares for me as more than a friend?"

Any amusement faded from Nora's gaze, replaced with irritation. "Don't be disingenuous. No man claims a child who isn't his unless he's mad for the woman. No man curses his own brother, dead in a grave, unless his loyalty lies with her. No man denies himself the joys of my Bordello for years, unless he is hopeful he'll have a chance with the woman of his dreams."

"Oh, Cormac," Niamh whispered, her hand over her mouth, as her eyes shone with wonder. She stared at Nora with a mixture of hope and abject terror. "I ... I fear Connor damaged me in ways I'll never overcome."

"Trust Cormac enough to share your fears, Niamh. That is one of the ways you can show your love."

That afternoon, Niamh left Maura napping under the watchful eye of her mother. The sun shone, and Niamh needed a walk to clear her head after speaking with the Madam. Niamh shook her head as she murmured, "Nora." For, although Nora ran the Bordello, Niamh had come to realize that Nora was much more than the owner of such a place. Niamh had pigeonholed Nora as much as any other townsfolk, so as not to consider her as a person worthy of her notice. Grimacing at her past attempt to make herself feel superior when she had been so vulnerable, Niamh fought guilt that her father had been the only one to see Nora as more than the Bordello's owner.

Niamh approached the Missouri, watching as the river flowed with deceptive calmness. How like the river she was. Keeping everything bottled up, until it burst from her in anger or tears. She closed her eyes, as she remembered the angry words she had spewed at Ardan the past summer. Even though it seemed he had forgiven her somehow, she knew she had to find a way to fully apologize.

Her gaze turned inward, as an unwanted memory surfaced. The present sounds faded away—of the river gurgling past, of the swallows chirping as they swooped overhead, and of the soft wind blowing.

"Connor," she whispered, *"I don't understand why you're so upset."* She

jolted as his hand slammed onto the table, rattling the crockery, although thankfully nothing careened onto the floor.

"You expect me to apologize?" he asked in a low and menacing voice, as he stalked toward her.

Niamh whimpered, holding a protective hand over her belly, as though she could guard her unborn child against the man approaching her. "Connor," she breathed, her eyes wild, as she lost her battle at not showing her fear.

"I had every right to teach you how you had displeased me last night, wife," he growled in a low voice. "You have no right questioning me."

"'Tisn't done," she whispered, shrieking and cowering against the wall as his hand rose in warning.

He nodded, as though satisfied by her response. "Don't tell me what is and isn't done, Niamh. I'm your husband, and I have the right to do whatever I please. If it pleases me that you never see your family again, that is what will happen. If it pleases me that my brother never darkens my doorstep again, that is what will occur. You have no right to question my authority."

"I don't understand," she whispered, tears silently coursing down her cheeks.

"When you married me, you became my property."

"I'm not a cow." Instantly she regretted her rash words, as he belted her sharply on her arm. She massaged it and tried to curl into herself.

"No, you're of less value. At least with a cow, I'd earn money from the milk and the cream. With you, I have to feed you and clothe you." He shook his head in disgust. "Should have known better than to marry."

Connor spun on his heel, grabbed his jacket off the back of the chair, and stormed from the house, leaving a devastated Niamh to contemplate her reality.

A man hollering to a friend jolted her into the present, staring at the Missouri again. From that moment in her marriage, her life had been a living hell. She had never known when Connor would find a reason to punish her again, and she lived in constant fear that he would follow through with his threat of keeping her away from her family or Cormac. She realized a deep-seated anger had taken root then, and it prevented her from apologizing for her errors. For, if her husband could never ask forgiveness for his brutality, then why should she for her petty outbursts?

Rubbing at her temples, she bowed her head and whispered, "Because I'm better than him. And worth ten Connor Aherns."

"Talking to yourself, Mrs. Ahern?" called out a supercilious voice.

"'Tis a finer person than yourself," Niamh snapped, as she faced Uriah Chaffee. Today he wore a pumpkin-colored suit with matching waistcoat. An unbecoming look for a man whose paunch continued to grow with Deirdre's fine cooking. Niamh battled a smile and acted as though she were coughing as she beheld him. "'Tis an interesting color you've chosen for a suit."

He preened in front of her, puffing out his chest and running a hand down the lapel of his suit coat. "It only goes to show how provincial you are. But then I suppose it can't be helped. When one is raised on a potato farm in a shack in Ireland, one can't expect you to have any sense of taste."

"Aye, true enough. Although I'm not color-blind," Niamh said, as she fought laughter at his affronted look. "I'd be careful if I were you, Mr. Chaffee. Deirdre might mistake you for a lost pumpkin and try to carve you up at Thanksgivin' time."

He glared at her, tapping his walking cane on the ground. "Is that a threat?"

"Nay," Niamh said. "Why should I feel any bitterness toward the man who attempted to steal my daughter away from me?" She shared a long look with the lawyer.

"I did my duty." He stood tall, his nose in the air, outraged at the implication he had acted with any impropriety.

"Nay, you acted to inflict harm and uncertainty. If not for Nora, I would never have known the full extent of the will."

He waved away her concern. "That is only ever shared between legal counsel. You should have instructed your lawyer to speak with me."

Niamh paused, her gaze filled with loathing and contempt. "An' where was I to find a lawyer in Fort Benton to represent me in October when the steamboats had stopped runnin'? Did you hope I'd have to go to Virginia City or Helena?" Her mind raced. "Or that Da would leave?" She shook her head, as though attempting to puzzle out a riddle that made no sense.

His satisfied smile tinged with cunning put her nerves on edge. "I'm afraid you'll never know, since that horrible woman interfered in affairs that were none of her business." He glowered in the direction of the Bordello. "And to think, your family, which is reputed to be the most respectable in town, has taken her in to live in your home. I'd be surprised if any man or woman would ever consider an O'Rourke sibling acceptable to marry ever again."

Niamh burst out laughing. "You do realize you are a complete hypocrite?" Her hazel eyes sparkled with mischief. "Nora told me all about your visits to see her Sirens." Her eyes glowed as he flushed an unbecoming beet red that clashed with his pumpkin-colored suit. "I'd think Mrs. Davies would be most interested in discovering your nighttime activities while she is at the hotel, reading her Bible, don't you?" She raised an eyebrow in challenge.

He clenched her wrist in a menacing grip, tight enough to leave a bruise. "You will leave my business with Mrs. Davies to me."

Niamh kicked him in the shin, wrenching free of his brutal hold. "Just as you will leave me alone, Mr. Chaffee. As you should have learned by now, you are the outsider in this town. No matter what you may believe about me and my marriage to Connor Ahern, I am well respected, as is my family. Few will take your side in any dispute."

She let out a deep breath, as she watched him storm away.

Niamh entered her parents' house, her gaze moving instinctively to her mother. When her mum smiled and nodded, Niamh relaxed. "Maura continues to recover?" she whispered.

"Yes, an' she's sleeping soundly just now. She fell asleep on Nora's lap again, but, after an hour, I thought it only fair to liberate the poor woman." Mary's hazel eyes twinkled with humor and a touch of mischief. "We're having an early dinner tonight, as we would like Nora to be present."

"I don't understand," Niamh said, as she took a deep breath of the redolent scents, closing her eyes with pleasure.

"We're finally celebrating Maggie's birthday," Mary said. "Deirdre is bringing a cake, and I've cooked something other than a stew." She squeezed Niamh's arm, frowning when she saw Niamh flinch. "Niamh?"

"I'm fine," Niamh said, as she moved to wash her hands and then to set the table. Soon her younger brothers had joined her, and they told her about their rambles, as they searched for anything of interest. They thought they'd easily find arrowheads used by the native tribes, but they'd yet to unearth one. "Perhaps this wasn't a hunting ground for them," Niamh said.

Oran rolled his eyes and sat with a huff. "Why must you be logical? I'm certain we'll find one. We just haven't been lucky."

Niamh smiled and shook her head. "Keep looking. You never know what you might find." She winked at Bryan and Henri, her smile broadening as they giggled.

Soon the entire family, including Nora and a recently arrived Dunmore, sat at the table for supper. Watching with thinly veiled amusement, Niamh observed how Dunmore participated in the conversation around him, while his focus never wavered from Maggie. Niamh fought envy at such devotion, even though Maggie seemed oblivious to it. After nearly the entire meal, where Niamh had tried to hold back her questions for Dunmore, they finally burst forth.

"Dunmore," she murmured, smiling as he looked at her. "I trust you left Mr. Ahern well the last you saw him."

Dunmore smiled cryptically. "Quite well." With a wry crook of his lips, he said, "Cormac seemed quite pleased with his decision and unregretful of the choices he had made."

"Oh," Niamh whispered, as she sat back, the remainder of her dinner unpalatable. "How … fortuitous for him to be so at ease."

"Yes. Finding peace can be the hardest endeavor for a man,"

Dunmore said with a nod, before joining a conversation with Ardan and Kevin.

Niamh sat in stupefied silence, her mind whirling from Dunmore's words. She dug her nails into her palm, as she knew she should be happy for Cormac. She should revel that he had found peace. That he was content. Instead she was bitterly angry. She wanted him as desperately unhappy as she was. And as eager to reunite with her as she was with him.

Her father scooted his chair from the table, the scraping sound causing conversation to falter, as everyone focused on Seamus. Unbidden, a tremendous pride filled her at the sight of her father, standing proud and commanding the respect of all who stared at him. Even though it was family and a few friends, she knew it was the same for the townsfolk. Her father was a remarkable man, for he was kind and just.

Seamus lifted his glass and smiled at everyone at the table. "I want to take a moment to thank everyone for bein' here." He smiled ruefully. "Aye, most of you are family an' have nowhere else to be." He paused as they chuckled. "But I'm glad we gather to celebrate our wee Maggie." His loving gaze turned to his youngest daughter. "We missed your birthday, lass, due to wee Maura's illness, but we would never want to go without celebrating you."

Seamus paused again, taking a deep breath. "For by celebrating Maggie, we will always celebrate the return of Mary too. Rather than that day bein' a day of mournin' for us, 'twill always be a day of thanksgiving, as it always should have been." He raised his glass, his eyes glistening with tears. "To Maggie, my beautiful daughter, returned to us."

"To Maggie!"

CHAPTER 9

The bright sunlight and crisp fall air beckoned to Niamh the following morning as she battled guilt for leaving Maura in her mother's care as she continued to recover. However, Niamh needed a few moments to consider all that had transpired in the past weeks. She walked away from her parents' house, intent on putting distance between her and the gossiping townsfolk. However, she shied away from heading up the small hill toward the cemetery. She had no desire to visit Connor's grave and knew she would eventually have to force herself to visit his grave for Maura's sake.

Instead she circled around toward the small stream that ran into the Missouri. Few birds lingered, as winter threatened, although a striking black-and-white magpie flitted from bush to bush. She stared into the gurgling shallow water of the creek and fought panic.

Closing her eyes, she took deep breaths, although the calm she prayed for remained elusive. How was she to do what the Madam suggested? How could she trust Cormac? Moreover, Dunmore was back, reporting Cormac was at peace with his decision. Anger filled her for a moment that he had so easily forgotten her; yet her anger was quickly replaced by despair.

As she envisioned her life here without him in it, her future was barren and lonely. Acknowledging that Cormac filled her days with warmth and hope, she feared how he would change were they to ever marry. For didn't men always change? She admitted to herself that the loss of Cormac as he was now would be worse than anything Connor ever did to her. For, without the hope of Cormac, she would feel truly hopeless for the first time in her life.

She dropped her head until her chin rested on her chest and listened to the sweet sounds of nature around her. The wind in the grass, the chirping of a distant chipmunk, the gurgle of water over the rocks. In that moment, she realized all she would continue to lose if she remained unable to marshal her courage. With a sigh, she turned for her parents' house, determined to find a way through her fear by the time Cormac returned in the spring.

As she walked back, she instinctively glanced in the direction of Cormac's vacant cabin, tripping on a rock as she saw a plume of woodsmoke emerging from the chimney. Heedless of what she would say when she arrived, she raced to his door, banging on it with her open palm. "Cormac!" she yelled. "Cormac!"

Her breath caught as the door opened, and he stood, tall and stoic in front of her. His hair was longer, beard thicker, and eyes more shadowed. "You came back," she breathed. "I feared I'd never see you again."

His blue eyes bored into hers, a glimmer of hope deep within. "You cared that I left?"

She pushed forward, smacking him on his arm. "Of course I did! How could you? After everything, how could you?" Suddenly a sob burst forth, and she held a hand to her mouth, as though she would be able to contain her emotions.

"Don't cry, Niamh," he murmured, moving awkwardly toward her. He raised his hands and then dropped them, uncertain if he should touch her or not. "I ... I don't know what to say."

"Tell me why you left. Why you abandoned me here." She ducked her head, as a sob burst out, and she was unsuccessful in tamping down her display of strong feelings.

"Abandoned you?" he frowned and shook his head. "You didn't

want me, Niamh. You've never wanted *me*." His eyes shone with the years' worth of disappointment. As though against his will, his hand rose to caress her cheek and to smooth away her tears.

"That's not true," she whispered, her gaze begging him to understand. "You told Dunmore you were at peace."

He smiled and nodded. "Of course I was. I was returning to Fort Benton. To my home." He paused, his blue eyes shining brightly with trepidation and yearning. "To you."

Niamh flushed and backed up a step, before forcing herself to still her evasive movements. "Cormac, we can't."

"Why?" he demanded. "Tell me why, dammit." His whispered voice, filled with entreaty and longing, provoked a shiver. His hand continued to stroke her shoulder, eliciting a subtle shuddering in her.

"You know why …" She closed her eyes, as though watching him was more than she could bear. "We killed him, Cormac."

His hand dropped from her, and she felt the absence of his touch, his warmth, as acutely as if he had pushed her away. "I know," he breathed. "It's a shame I live with every day." He paused. "Although I find it difficult to regret you are free of him."

"How could we marry, knowing what we did caused him to die?" she asked, as she moved to a chair and sat. She bowed forward as a sob emerged. "Don't you realize I'll never be free of him? He lives on …" She shook her head.

"In Maura," Cormac murmured.

"No, never in her," Niamh said in a fierce voice. "Maura is sweet and kind and good. Everything Connor wasn't." She paused as she took a deep breath and swiped at her cheeks with her fingers. "I hear his taunting voice every time I try something new. Every time I hope, I hear him mocking me that I deserve all the misery I suffer." She shook her head and flushed, as though mystified she had revealed such a personal sorrow.

"Ah, my Niamh," Cormac said, as he knelt in front of her, gripping her hands. "That's his shame, love. Not yours." He flushed at calling her *love* but didn't recall the word. His eyes glowed with the deep emotion. "I hope that, someday soon, you hear another voice, telling you how beautiful and brilliant you are." He squeezed her wrists and froze as she gasped in pain. "Niamh?"

She tugged on her hands, but he wouldn't free them. "'Tis nothing, Cormac."

When he stared at her as though he had heard that too many times in the past to believe such lies now, her shoulders slumped, and she waited as he pushed up the sleeve to her dress. Her right wrist and forearm were smooth and free of blemish. With a confused frown, he tugged on the other sleeve and froze at the purple bruising in the shape of fingers. "Niamh?"

Grabbing his arm, she shook her head. "No. You aren't racing out of here like a madman."

"Someone hurt you," he rasped, glaring at the bruises. The word *again* sat heavily between them.

"Aye," she whispered. "But I was able to free myself." Unable to prevent a pride-filled smile from bursting forth, she met Cormac's surprised gaze. "Mr. Chaffee was shocked a woman would fight back."

"He'll have his day of reckoning," Cormac whispered in a menacing voice.

"Aye, but not today." Her hand rose to trace his cheek, as she stared deeply into his eyes. "You were worried about me," she whispered.

"Always. Forever," he vowed.

She gazed at him with yearning and wonder, her body arching toward him. Just as she was about to kiss him, she jerked away. "No! We can't. This is wrong."

Cormac groaned, dropping his forehead to her shoulder. "Why, when we care for each other?" The soft exhalation of his breath elicited a shiver, and he turned his head to kiss her neck.

"If he hadn't seen us kissing, he wouldn't have stormed away. He wouldn't have gone to the Bordello and died," Niamh breathed. She raised her gaze to meet Cormac's, hers filled with shame and longing.

"If he had treated you like the precious woman you are, you would never have considered kissing me," he whispered. His gaze clouded. "Besides, we know what things were like after August. You'd never have reconciled with him."

She raised her hand, her fingers covering his lips, and shook her head. "No. I don't want to talk about that."

Cormac stared at her a long time, his gaze tormented. Finally he nodded. "Fine, for now we can act as though the events of August never occurred. But, someday, you will have to face what happened, Niamh."

A tear leaked down her cheek, and she rested her head against his chest. "All I feel is ashamed, and I'm so tired of feeling that way."

"*Shh*," he whispered in her ear, as his arms gently banded around her. Although she stiffened in his arms when he first touched her, she eventually relaxed in his embrace. "You're safe, Niamh. You'll always be safe with me."

L ater that day, Cormac stood on the O'Rourke's back stoop, battling nerves and a sense of panic. Although he desperately wanted to marry Niamh, he feared she would never come to care for him as he did her. He didn't know if he could handle a life lived in a marriage with one-sided affection. Ducking his head, he admitted to himself he would take whatever crumbs of affection Niamh would offer him and would pray that she would come to care for him with even the smallest portion of her love.

He stood tall and rapped on the back door. With a confident smile, he nodded at Mary, who appeared shocked by his appearance. "Mrs. O'Rourke," he murmured deferentially. "May I come in?"

"Cormac!" she exclaimed, throwing her arms around him. "Oh, you've returned. You returned now. I feared ..." She grabbed his arm and pulled him inside. "I feared for how Niamh suffered without you."

His eyes shone with that morsel of information at Niamh's feelings for him. "I realized running away never solved any problems."

She cupped his cheeks and beamed at him, as though she were his proud mother. "You're right, but few men have the ability to admit when they've been wrong." She gave his cheeks a gentle pat. "Good for you, my lad." She moved to the stove to pour him a cup of coffee and motioned for him to sit at the table.

Seamus entered the kitchen, his gaze focused on a slip of paper in his hands. "Love, who was that at the door?" he asked absently.

"Me," Cormac said.

Seamus's head jerked up, and his blue eyes sparkled with delight. "Cormac," he breathed. "You came back to us with Dunmore." When Cormac jerked his head yes, Seamus shared a relieved smile with his wife. "But 'tis not us who you've come to see." Turning toward the connecting door, he bellowed, "Niamh!"

"Shay, what if Maura was asleep?" Mary admonished, with a hand down his arm.

Shrugging, Seamus murmured, "Then she'd wake up, fuss, and fall back asleep again." He pulled Mary into his arms and kissed the top of her head. "'Tis too wondrous a day to tiptoe around. 'Tis one to be lived out loud."

Cormac frowned, as though pondering Seamus's pronouncement, but forgot about it the moment he saw Niamh. She appeared much as she did when she had come to his cabin, although her gaze showed her to be at peace, rather than tormented. He longed to rush to her, to take her in his arms, and to soothe himself with her presence. Instead he remained across the room, filled with longing. "Niamh," he murmured.

"Cormac," she breathed. "You've returned then."

He fought a bemused smile, as she pretended this was their reunion, and nodded. "I found I had left something important behind in Fort Benton."

Standing tall and with a proud tilt to her chin, Niamh stared at him with defiance. "Your oxen?"

Cormac burst out laughing. "Aye, I left my oxen here, you daft woman. But they aren't why I returned." He took a step toward her, watching for any sign of fear or hesitancy on her part. "I returned because I knew I didn't want to live without you. The moment I left, I was filled with grief at the thought I might never see you again,

Niamh. And I was filled with fear at what you might feel compelled to do to keep Maura safe."

Any teasing had faded, and he stared at her with ardent solemnity. "Let me be the man who cares for you and Maura. Let me be the one you turn to when you need help. Let me be the man who you gift with your smiles and laughter. Please marry me."

Niamh stared at him with wide stunned eyes at his proposal, her chest heaving, as though she had just run across the plains. Her gaze flickered to her parents, and Seamus ushered a quietly sobbing Mary from the room. When they were alone, Niamh whispered, "What will you do when you are angry?"

Cormac reared back as though she had just backhanded him. He closed his eyes, took a deep breath, and met her petrified gaze. "If you don't know me by now, Niamh, you'll never know who I am. But I'll give you the words you need." He paused. "I promise I will never strike you or Maura. Ever. I will never speak to you in a degrading way that batters your confidence in ways physical blows never can." He took another deep breath. "I might yell when I get angry, but it will never be at you. It will be at fate, at the men I work with, at my slow-moving oxen."

"I'm not worth yelling at?" she asked.

"Oh, love," he whispered, as he took a step closer, cradling her cheeks in his palms. His ardent gaze bore into hers. "You are precious beyond words. And it's because you are precious that you should never be yelled at." He waited for a moment before murmuring, "I promise I will do everything I can to ease you of your fear of me. Of men."

She smiled and pushed herself into his embrace. "I don't fear you, Cormac. I fear how you might change once we marry. Once you control me."

He chuckled. "Ah, my little love, soon you will come to understand that I have no desire for control. I yearn for respect, admiration, and love." His eyes shone with hope at his last words.

"As do I," she whispered, holding him closer. "Yes, I'll marry you, Cormac." She wriggled until she was out of his tight hold and staring into his gaze, with only his hands on her shoulders. Although she appeared afraid, she battled her fear and whispered, "There's no one else I would ever agree to marry. Only you, Cormac."

∽

A rdan stood staring into space, his gaze distant as he looked out the polished windows facing Front Street of Fort Benton. His hair hung longer than when he had married Deirdre a few months ago, although not as long as Declan's before he had departed for Saint Louis. His beard was neatly trimmed, and he looked startlingly like a younger version of Da.

Now that it was nearly November, the streets were mainly quiet, and the café had business for breakfast and lunch. He and Deirdre preferred to spend almost every dinner with his family, with the rare night at home for the two of them. Although he missed working with his brothers and father, the dinners kept him in the loop with store activities, and he relished running the business with his wife. With a contented sigh, he flicked the lock on the front door of the empty café and spun on his heels to return to the kitchen to help wash dishes and to flirt with his wife.

He stilled when he saw Niamh standing a few feet inside the café, having entered through the kitchen. "You're as quiet as a cat," he said, as he studied her. He set down the rag he used to swipe down the tables and crossed his arms over his chest, waiting to hear what had brought Niamh by.

"I found I needed to speak with you," she blurted out.

"Aye?" he said, with a tilt of his head.

"I need to apologize."

"What's happened?" He took a frantic step in the direction of the kitchen. "Deir?" he called out.

"I'm fine," his wife's distant voice yelled back.

Niamh glared at him with momentary indignation. "I never would hurt Deirdre." She huffed out a sigh and closed her eyes. "I meant to be apologizin' to you, and I'm about to start another fight." She opened her eyes to find him watching her with a glint of amusement in his gaze. "'Tisn't funny, Ard."

"Of course it is," he said with a wry smile. "'Tis how we've always been." He sobered. "Until recently."

She nodded and gripped her hands together. "Aye," she whispered. "I'm sorry." When he made no move to accept her apology, she blurted out, "I'm sorry I acted so horribly to you when you first showed interest in Deirdre. I'm sorry I ever thought you would have hurt her." She closed her eyes. "I'm sorry I was jealous."

"Jealous?" he whispered, as he inched forward.

She met his confused gaze with resignation. "I knew I'd never have a man as good as you, who would be as concerned and eager to see me. And I lashed out." She ducked her head. "I'm sorry, Ardan."

"Oh, you wee *eejit*," he breathed, as he tugged her into his arms. He rocked her from side to side as he used to do when they were children, heralding a memory she had buried after they thought their mother had died, and Niamh had refused comfort from everyone. Rather than push away as he expected, she clung to him. "You've always had that man. You never paid attention."

"I am now," she said in a soft voice. She squeezed him and then backed up a step. "I've spoken with Cormac. He's back." She nodded, as he stared at her with delight, unable to hide the wonder in her gaze. "We'll marry."

"Oh, Niamh, finally," he breathed, pulling her close to swing her in a circle. At her startled shriek, he laughed. After setting her down, he stared into her shining eyes, filled with joy and anticipation, no fear or trepidation visible. "Finally you'll know what it is to be cherished."

"By a husband, yes," she said. "You forgive me?"

"I forgave you months ago, Niamh," he said, smiling when she gaped at him. "I only hope you can forgive me."

"For what?" she whispered. "You've never done anything to harm me." She ducked her head at admitting her greatest fear.

"And I hope I never will." He brushed back a wisp of her hair. "I vowed to keep Maggie safe, but I didn't have the ability to see how much you suffered." He clamped his jaw in anger. "If I'd known, Niamh ..." He broke off, shaking his head.

"Then the sheriff would have visited for you, and Deirdre would be asleep in a lonely bed. I'm trying to accept it all worked out as it should have."

"Aye," Ardan murmured. "An' I pray, every night, that you feel no guilt for being free of such a man and for finding love with his brother."

A tear coursed down her cheek, as she gazed at her beloved eldest brother. "You pray for me?"

Smiling, he swiped away her tear. "Of course I do. You're precious to me, Niamh." He pulled her close for a moment and then kissed her head. "Come. Let's tell Deir your news. She'll be over the moon for you."

~

Mary knocked on Nora's bedroom door in the late afternoon, waiting as she heard the soft scrape of a chair and then gentle footsteps. Mary smiled sardonically. For all the woman was a Bordello owner, she was quite genteel. When Nora opened the door, Mary's smile was filled with warmth. "Hello, Nora. I did not see you at breakfast and wanted to ensure you had all you needed."

Nora chuckled. "Every day you visit my room, and every day it's the same. I worked until this morning, had breakfast at the Bordello, and came here to sleep." She paused as she saw a triumphant gleam in Mary's eyes. "What's occurred?" She motioned for Mary to enter her room. After Mary sat on the desk chair, Nora perched on the bed.

Mary stared at her with a wondrous joy. "Cormac returned. He realized his error in leaving Niamh and came back to her. He wants to marry her and to keep her and Maura safe."

Nora closed her eyes, as though saying a silent prayer. "Oh, what marvelous news." She stared at Mary with unveiled envy. "You and your daughter are most fortunate."

Frowning with befuddlement, Mary shook her head. "I don't understand what you mean."

"You have the ability to provoke a deep, abiding loyalty and love in a man. Few women can." Nora smiled. "And you chose good men."

Mary flushed. "Well, we both had a marriage that taught us what we never wanted to suffer again." She shared a long look with Nora. "I know you've spoken with Niamh. I know she has seemed calmer, less conflicted, after you speak with her. As a mother, 'tis hard to admit she might need someone else's counsel, other than my own. However, my greatest wish is to see Niamh happy and free of the burden of her past. Thank you, Nora, for all you've done while you've been here."

Nora flushed. "I've done little."

"No, you've done everything. You ensured Niamh wouldn't lose Maura. You ensured Niamh continued to heal and continued to believe that a future with a man like Cormac was possible, even after all she'd suffered." Mary shared a long look with Nora. "Thank you."

"You have it all backward, Mary. There is little I wouldn't do to help the O'Rourkes. Seamus showed me tremendous loyalty and friendship when most people treated me like I was little more than a piece of garbage for my profession."

Mary stiffened at the mention of her husband and then relaxed. "Seamus reassured me that you were only ever friends." At the answering affirmation in Nora's gaze, any residual doubt eased. "I've always wanted to thank you for befriending him when he felt so alone. When I wasn't here to comfort him. He's not a man to be without a woman's gentling care."

"He was, every day, until you returned, Mary. Every woman he spoke with was a poor substitute for the woman he wanted. Never doubt that," Nora said.

Mary smiled and rose. "I thank you again, Nora. Although I know you are eager to leave for home, I would ask that you remain here until the wedding. I wouldn't want Mr. Chaffee or the sheriff to believe they had cause to create any more mischief."

Nora chuckled and rose, impulsively hugging Mary. "Of course. It's no imposition, and Ezra always knows where to find me."

Mary returned the hug and then slipped from the room to find her husband.

~

Later that night Niamh sat at the large kitchen table, warmed by the stove and by her memories of Cormac's return. His words. His promises. Unlike Connor, she believed Cormac would keep his promises to her. In the years she had known him, he had never broken his word to her. She sighed, rubbing her forehead, as she fought daydreaming about what it would have been like to have married Cormac from the beginning. To have had Connor visit sporadically.

Against her will, images of a home filled with laughter, joy, and harmony filled her mind. Unable to cease her imaginings, she closed her eyes, while a small smile burst forth. Cormac hugging her from behind, while she was large with a baby. Cormac laughing at something she said. Cormac helping with whatever she needed. Always was there happiness and a sense of security.

Niamh took a stuttering breath, saying a silent prayer that her imaginings turned into reality. For her girlish dreams of the past had turned into a hell on earth she never wanted to relive. With a start, she turned to the icebox to find her father attempting to close it softly. "Da?" she asked in a low voice.

"Forgive me, love," he said, as he poured a glass of milk. "Your mum wanted her glass of milk but had no desire to leave the warmth of her bed." He smiled with chagrin and love. "Thus, I became her servant."

Niamh smiled, a warmth filling her at the love and devotion in his gaze. "You'd never really complain about helping Mum."

Seamus smiled and shook his head. "Although I am sorry to have disturbed you, wee Niamh. You seemed to be havin' a lovely wakin' dream."

She flushed and ducked her head.

After Seamus returned the milk jar to the icebox and set the glass on the counter, he moved to sit beside her. "Niamh?" he asked in a soft voice. "Are you well?" When she remained quiet, he whispered, "Are you certain you want to marry Cormac?"

Niamh froze, her gaze filled with terror. "Are you tellin' me that I shouldn't?" When her father remained quiet, she gripped his arm. "Do you know somethin' about him you aren't tellin' me? Suspect somethin' like you did with Connor?" Her head moved back and forth as though disavowing the idea her family would willingly allow her to reenter another hellish marriage again without battling for her. "Please, fight for me, Da. Believe I'm worth it."

"Oh, Niamh," Seamus gasped, as he cupped her cheeks. "You always were. But you'd run off with that scoundrel and spent days and nights with him." His gaze was filled with impotent fury. "I've always felt I had no choice but to let you marry him. Even though I never wanted you to." He paused and closed his eyes. "I always wished you'd chosen Cormac."

Niamh hunched forward. "Why didn't you speak to me before my marriage to Connor? Why didn't you try to change my mind? Act like a father?"

Seamus cringed backward, as though she had stabbed him with a knife. "I've always known I've failed you, Niamh. After the death of Mary. Or the separation." He sighed and rubbed his temple. "On the steamboat, your brothers and I tried to protect you, but you outsmarted us, finding ways to have trysts with Connor. I was naive and trusting in my belief that Connor was an honorable man. That he would never act in such a way as to force you into doing anything. I was wrong."

Seamus's cobalt-blue eyes gleamed with anger, fear, and hatred as he stared at a spot on the tabletop. "When I discovered you missin' an' learned you'd run off with the two Ahern lads ..." He stopped, closing his eyes, as he took a deep breath. "I wanted to murder."

"Da," Niamh whispered, as a tear tracked down her cheek. "I wasn't worth such concern."

"No, Niamh, you were an' you are. The tragedy is that you've never believed it. An' you sold yourself short to the worst sort of man the first time." He took another deep breath. "I have no fears for you with

Cormac. He's nothin' like his brother. He's honorable an' good." Seamus stared for a long moment into Niamh's hazel eyes. "But he'll not want you to hide. Not behind your daughter. Not behind your fears. He'll want the real woman. The whole woman. An' I fear you'll find that terrifyin', my Niamh."

Niamh's eyes rounded as her breaths emerged as pants, as though battling a panic attack. "Da," she gasped.

"Aye, love," he murmured, pulling her close, so she rested against his shoulder. He wrapped his strong arms around her, rocking her in place. "You must let him see the real woman. Not the woman you show the town. Or your brothers. But the real woman, with her hurts and her dreams and her fears. The woman who cries, laughs, and sings out of tune. The real you, Niamh. For, if you don't, your marriage to Cormac will be another form of hell. And, this time, 'twill be of your own making."

She clung to her father for many long minutes. "'Tis almost as terrifyin' as anything Connor did."

"Aye," Seamus whispered, as he kissed her head. "Because, this time, you must trust and love Cormac. And that makes you all the more vulnerable."

Niamh shivered at his last words, taking comfort in his presence, as she considered all her father had said.

CHAPTER 10

Two evenings after returning to Fort Benton, Cormac opened his door, silently berating himself for being a fool. He had hoped for Niamh to be here, so he imagined he heard a gentle tapping. With a sigh, he looked outside, expecting to see nothing more than darkness and stars in the distant sky. Instead a figure shrouded in a black cloak huddled on his stoop. "Niamh?" he breathed.

"Please, let me in," she whispered.

He gripped her arm, pulling her inside, before he kicked the door shut. Without thinking, he latched the door and then waited for her to ease off her cloak. However, she remained obscured from view by the heavy garment. "Come, love. Let's take this off you. I have a fine fire built tonight." He reached forward, stilling his movement as she flinched at his soft touch. "Niamh?"

The hood of the cloak slipped free, exposing her lustrous auburn hair, shot red tonight in the soft candlelight glow. "I … I thought I could do this. I must do this."

"*Shh*, love, there is no *must* between us." He ran his hands over her arms. "What are you thinking?" When she shook in front of him, he whispered, "Feeling?"

"I'm so embarrassed," she blurted out. Her gaze flew to his in mortification, as he unwittingly laughed. "I should go."

"No!" Cormac cried out, gripping her arm. They stumbled, and he landed near her against the door. Their breaths emerged as pants, and he rested his arms on the sturdy pine, easing his weight off her. "Forgive me for crushing you, my love," he whispered. His head dipped forward, kissing her forehead and cheek, before backing away. "I would never mean to scare you."

She stared at him, wide-eyed, her chest heaving.

"Niamh, forgive me," he repeated, his eyes filled with agonizing regret. "I know ... I know how you suffered, and I would never harm you. On everything I am, I swear to you."

She took a step toward him, her gaze filled with wonder. "I know you, Cormac," she whispered. "How is it that I feel as though I'm seeing you for the first time?"

He flinched. "I tripped. I ..."

Shaking her head, Niamh held her fingers to his lips to prevent him from babbling any more excuses. "No, love." She flushed as she said the endearment. "No, *a shíorghrá*, no more apologies." She blinked as she fought tears. "You should expect me to apologize to you."

"Never," he rasped, his lips kissing her fingers.

"I'm so afraid, Cormac, but I realize 'tisn't you I'm afraid of. 'Tis my memories. 'Tis everything but you." She reached for the tie at her neck and released her cloak, shrugging her shoulders, so it slipped off to land at her feet. "I ... I need to know I'll be a proper wife to you before we marry. I fear ..." She ducked her head as a tear leaked out.

"If all I ever did was hold you in my arms as you slept beside me, I would know I had heaven within my grasp," he rasped. "I will never want more than you can offer me, Niamh. I will never hurt you."

Her smile was luminous and filled with trust as she took a step toward him. Reaching forward, she traced her fingers through his beard. "You've told me that before, but I learned long ago that words had little meaning. Actions have significance." She saw understanding in his gaze. She leaned forward, kissing his cheek. "Tonight, rather than pin me to the door, kissing me, and making me feel weak and insignificant, you made me feel cherished." She kissed his jaw. "Adored." A kiss to his neck. "Revered."

He tipped his head back, a groan escaping as she wreaked havoc on him. "Ah, Niamh, you are all those things to me. And so much more."

"Hold me, Cormac. I won't break, and I need to feel your arms around me." She nodded, meeting his searching gaze. With a sigh, she eased into his arms, nestling her head under his chin. "'Tis where I should have always been," she murmured.

When he remained quiet, she tipped her head back to stare at him, as she fought doubts. "Cormac?"

His eyes glinted, as though he fought tears, and he traced callused fingers over her silky cheeks. "Yes, my darling," he whispered, a moment before kissing her softly. Breaking the kiss so only a hairbreadth was between them, he said, "Where I've always wanted you."

He maintained a light hold as he felt her battle freezing up. He ran his hands over her back, again and again in soft caresses. "You are enough as you are, my darling. I would never want you to be other than you are."

Unbidden, a sob burst forth, and she struggled to free herself from his hold. "No," she gasped. "I don't want …"

"*Shh*, love," he soothed. Although he had released her, he remained in front of her and continued to run his hands over her. "Don't hide from me. Please."

She pushed forward, into his arms, burying her face against his chest, as deep sobs burst forth. "How can you care for me when I hated your brother so much at the end?" she gasped. "How?"

He kissed her head, rocking her gently side to side, as she would have done for Maura had she held Maura in her arms. "You're not unloving, Niamh. He pushed you away. He pushed you to loathe him." He kissed her head again. "If he hadn't hurt you in August"—Cormac paused as he swallowed, his hold on her tightening—"I doubt you would ever have considered kissing me."

She backed away and gave him a rueful smile. "I fear that isn't true." She flushed. "I'd dreamed of you for a long time, Cormac."

His eyes flared with yearning.

Niamh closed her eyes, as though with shame and regret. "I was a foolish young woman, desperate to feel loved. Connor knew how to exploit my emotions, whereas you were patient and kind. I fell for flamboyance rather than substance. I'm sorry."

He shook his head. "You're not to blame, Niamh. I should have fought for you. I should have spoken up." He ducked his head. "I should never have let you marry him."

She flushed as she whispered, "I thought, once I spent the night with him, you'd never want me again."

His gaze blazed with passion and longing. "Nothing could make me not want you, Niamh. Never forget that."

After a long moment of silence, only broken by the crackling of wood in the stove, she whispered, "Will you hold me? All night long?"

"Gladly." He kissed her chastely before gripping her hand and leading her in the direction of his comfortable bed. "As long as you reassure me that no O'Rourke will beat down that door, intent on murder."

She laughed. "No. Mum understands why I came here tonight, and her word rules. She'll keep everyone calm."

He ran a soothing hand over her head and shoulders, before pausing with his fingers on the buttons of her dress. "I will sleep with my trousers on, love, but I want you to be comfortable. Will you sleep in your shift, or do you want to remain in your dress and corset?"

Niamh took a deep breath. "Just my shift," she breathed, her cheeks a fiery red. Her fingers worked on the buttons on the front of her dress but shook so badly that she was unable to free any of them.

"*Shh*, darling, you'll tear them off," he teased, as he leaned down to kiss her on her nose. "Let me help you." He freed each button, his breath catching as he inched her dress over her shoulders and hips. He let out a deep breath when it pooled at her feet. "I feel a fool for not noticing, but you aren't wearing a corset."

She flushed crimson and shook her head. "I know that makes me a harlot but no."

Cormac made a growl of displeasure and cupped her face. "Never speak of yourself to me in that way again, Niamh. Any word against you is against me, don't you understand?"

She gazed at him in astonishment at his words and dumbly shook her head.

"Any harm against you, harms me. Any pain you suffer, pains me. Any slight against you is against me too." He took a deep breath. "When I asked you to marry me, I didn't do it to appease the gossips of this town or to ensure you would always have Maura." He gazed deeply into her awestruck hazel eyes. "I asked you because I can't imagine life without you. I love you, Niamh."

She opened and closed her mouth a few times like a fish out of water, before a tear trickled down her cheek. "I'm afraid I'm unfamiliar with your kind of love."

Staring at her with infinite patience, Cormac smiled. "No, you aren't. Your parents shared with you this kind of devotion. You know what this is like."

Rather than agree or disagree, Niamh pushed forward into his embrace, holding him close. "Hold me, Cormac. Never let me go."

"Never, my love. Never."

Niamh woke in fits and starts. A warm arm wrapped around her middle, and she felt safe for the first time upon waking in a man's arms since … Her mind grappled with the notion, and she couldn't recall the last time she had felt like this. She fought waking, as she clung to the sensation of security, but soon her eyes flickered open. Rather than the room she shared with Maura at her parents' home, she stared at a stove and table with two chairs around it. A cup with a plate with a half-eaten dinner sat on the table, and she lurched up, shaking.

"Niamh, *shh*, all is well," Cormac murmured, as he ran a hand over her back.

Looking over her shoulder, she gazed at Cormac, his eyes barely opened as he watched her. "I'm sorry I didn't do the dishes last night. I should have cleaned up. I should never have thought to interrupt you or to sleep. I'm sorry for my self-importance—"

Her words broke off as Cormac covered her lips with his hand. "Stop." He sighed as she flinched at his firm tone. "Don't apologize, Niamh. Those are my dishes, and I'll wash them. I've been washing them for years."

When he dropped his hand, she flinched, and he frowned, focused on the fear in her gaze.

"Oh, Niamh, please tell me that he didn't stoop so low," he whispered, breaking off what more he would have said, as though he fought rage and sorrow, his voice thickened with deep emotion. He ran a hand over her shoulder, before urging her to rest beside him again. His arm wrapped around her, holding her close in a cherishing rather than a threatening way.

"I'm sorry, Cormac," she whispered, then winced at apologizing after he had asked her not to. "I've ruined our time together." She shivered as he kissed the back of her neck.

"No, my Niamh, you haven't. He's intruded again, and I'd prefer for him to remain a distant memory. But we will overcome this, Niamh. I know we will."

She wriggled around until she could face him and stared deeply into his eyes. Her fingers tangled in his long brown hair. "How can you believe I'm worth the trouble?"

His brows furrowed as he stared deeply into her hazel eyes. "*Trouble?* Is that what you believe you are?" He leaned forward, kissing her softly and sighing with relief as he felt her relax. "Beloved." He kissed her nose. "Precious." A kiss to her soft skin below her right ear. "Treasured." A kiss below her left ear. He ran his nose and lips over her cheek, eliciting a shiver of excitement, rather than fear.

She grabbed his face, holding it as he hovered over her, on the verge of kissing her lips. She gazed deeply into his eyes, seeing all he said. Arching up, she kissed him and wrapped her arms around his neck to pull him down to her.

Cormac groaned, kissing her deeply. His hands tangled in her hair, and he held his weight off her on his elbows. "Niamh," he rasped, when he broke the kiss, his mouth kissing her cheeks, jaw, and neck. "How I want you."

"Then have me," she gasped, as she arched up into his touch.

With one last kiss, he groaned, this time in regret, and flopped onto his back. "No." One arm rested over his eyes, and he panted as though he had just run a mile.

Feeling like she had just fallen through ice into the frozen Missouri, Niamh shivered. Rather than lean into Cormac, she wrapped her arms around herself, as she searched for the fortitude to rise and to walk home. She closed her eyes, dreading the questioning stares. The hopeful glances from her parents and Maggie, as they dreamed of a joyous union between Cormac and her. Clinging to the sense of icy numbness, Niamh pushed herself from the bed and found her dress.

"Where are you going?" Cormac asked in a husky voice.

"There's no reason for me to stay," she said, her back to him, as she deftly buttoned her dress, sighing with relief when she had another barrier between her and the man she would marry. "I must return to check on Maura." She turned to gaze at him, paling at the disappointment and hurt she saw in his expression.

"Will you always use her as an excuse when you run away from me?" he whispered.

She stood near the doorway, shuddering and terrified, her hands pleating the fabric of her skirts. Although her mind ordered her to run, her feet remained rooted in place. "Maura is my daughter."

"Yes, and my niece. I love her with all my heart too, Niamh. But you and I both know she is well cared for at your parents' house. She is cherished there." He waited for her to say something else, but she swayed in place and stared at him in silent misery. "You don't believe me," he whispered, a note of incredulity in his voice. "After all the time we've spent together, still you doubt."

"Words are the cheapest commodity," Niamh gasped out and then went ghost white as her eyes widened. "I didn't mean to say that."

Cormac sat up at a glacially slow pace, his gaze on Niamh the entire time. He watched as she took a step closer to the door as his feet hit the floor. Rather than reach for her, as he desired, he placed his palms on his muscled thighs. "They may be, but they can be as powerful as any fist, Niamh." He waited for her to meet his gaze. "When I promise you that I will never raise a hand against you in anger, I am speaking my truth. When I tell you that I will honor you until the day I die, that is a vow I make to myself as well as to you. When I swear my love for you, that is a truth written on my heart."

Tears trickled down her cheeks, as she gazed into the passionate sincerity of his gaze. "You didn't want me," she cried out. "I offered you me, and you said no!"

Cormac lurched off the bed, and she shrieked, backing up until she hit the door. He held her gaze as he approached her slowly with the caution of a wild horse tamer. "Oh, love, you have it all muddled in your head again." He paused a foot away from her. "Let me hold you and comfort you, so I can explain. Please, love."

She pushed forward, into his embrace, sobbing into his chest. "Why didn't you want me?" she cried over and over.

When she had finally calmed, Cormac eased her back to the bed, where he sat and tugged her, so she was cradled on his lap. "Feel better?" he murmured, as he kissed her forehead and rubbed circles on her back.

"You're treating me like Maura," she grumbled.

"Perhaps," he whispered, a hint of laughter in his voice. He waited until she tilted her head and could meet his gaze. "How could you not feel how much I wanted you when we kissed?" He smiled when he saw a healthy blush rise on her cheeks. He ran a hand over her disheveled hair, cradling her head in his large palm. "I've wanted you from the moment I first saw you."

Her gaze was filled with doubt, confusion, and hope. "I don't understand, Cormac."

He paused a moment, before lowering his head and kissing her softly. "When you come to my bed for us to make love together, I want it to be just the two of us." He closed his eyes. "I know that might be impossible, but that is my hope." His blue eyes blazed with fervent intensity as he looked at her again. "I want to know you want *me*. Not that you are trying to forget. Or battling your fears. Or proving something to yourself."

She froze in his arms, her eyes widening with horror the more he spoke. "Cormac," she breathed with shame. "I'm sorry."

"*Shh*, my love. I didn't say any of this to make you feel bad." He took a deep breath. "I want you. I'll want you forever. But I will wait until you are ready and until you want me the same way."

"Why are you so patient with me?" Her fingers played through his beard and then his hair.

"I know you don't believe me, but you're worth it. One day, you'll believe it too."

She shivered, huddling closer to him on his lap, no longer eager to return to the safety of her parents' home. For now, all she wanted was to be in Cormac's embrace.

~

That evening, Niamh sat beside Cormac, as her mum and Maggie served supper. Nora and Dunmore had joined them, and the table was crowded again, reminiscent of the time in the summer before Declan, Eamon, and Finn had departed for Saint Louis. She watched Deirdre giving her and Cormac furtive looks, and she smiled encouragingly. However, Deirdre blushed and looked down, as though embarrassed and unwilling to celebrate Cormac sitting beside her.

Niamh set her hand by her leg and reached out her fingers, stroking the side of Cormac's hand. She relaxed as he moved his larger hand to cover hers and then to link their fingers. "Thank you for coming to dinner tonight," she whispered into his ear.

"Only a fool turns down a home-cooked meal," he said, a teasing glint in his gaze. "Besides, your father said I had to be here for an announcement he has to make."

Niamh watched Cormac for a moment, noting that his glance never left Dunmore watching her sister, Maggie. "He's protective," she murmured.

"That's not all he is," he said with a soft chuckle. "He's smitten but knows there's nothing to do about it yet." He shook his head when Niamh tensed. "And there's nothing for you to do either, Niamh. They'll discover what they need to in time."

Niamh squeezed his hand. "I hope he understands it might be a few years. She just turned eighteen."

Whispering soft sounds meant to soothe her, he said, "Of course he does. He cares, Niamh. He won't hurt her." He paused. "Every time he goes to Virginia City, he tries to discover where Jacques is. To ensure he is far away from here."

Niamh's gaze flew to behold Dunmore, now in earnest conversation with her da. "Oh, how wonderful."

"He's a good man." Cormac kissed her brow. "Trust me." At the shaky exhalation of her breath, his gaze held hers, and it appeared he would recall his words. However, she raised a hand to brush over his cheek and smiled tremulously.

"I will believe you. For I do trust you, Cormac." She flushed at the deep flash of emotion in his gaze. She nodded to the head of the table. "My da's watching us."

"That's because he's delighted to see us together and to see us finally happy," Cormac said in a raspy voice, thick with emotion. He glanced in Seamus's direction and then frowned. He leaned over to continue to whisper in his fiancée's ear. "Why does Deirdre look at me with suspicion?"

Niamh shrugged and shook her head. "I don't know. She smiled and gave me a hug when I told her that we were to marry, after I spoke with Ardan, but she seemed reluctant to be truly happy for me." She gazed deeply into Cormac's beautiful blue eyes. "Do you think she fears I can never be happy?"

"No, love," he whispered, caressing her cheek. "Never that."

Seamus cleared his throat and knocked on the table, effectively silencing all conversations. He stared at everyone present with a proud gleam in his eye, while holding Mary's hand. "'Tis my most wonderful honor, and with great joy, that I announce to the family that our beautiful Niamh is to marry Cormac in early December."

Pandemonium ensued after the announcement, with Maggie shrieking her joy and bouncing out of her chair to hug Niamh and Cormac. The younger boys enveloped them in hugs, while Aileen pulled Niamh close for a long moment, whispering, "I wish you the greatest joy, Niamh." Kevin held Niamh close, breathing into her ear, "I promise I'll keep you safe this time."

Niamh backed away from Kevin, brushing away a tear that coursed down her cheek. "You won't have to, Kevin. Cormac will." She squeezed her brother's hand, as though to take away any sting from her words. "I don't blame you." She took in a deep breath. "That time is over, and soon we will have so much to celebrate."

Nora approached, and Niamh watched her with mild trepidation in her gaze. After a moment's hesitation, Niamh opened her arms to pull her into a hug too. "Thank you, Nora," Niamh whispered. "Thank you for helping to keep Maura safe."

Nora backed away, her hands gripping Niamh's arms. "You kept your daughter safe, Niamh. You ensured she was healthy and well. I merely changed my address for a little while." She stared for a long moment into Niamh's eyes. "I wish you the happiness you were so long denied, the wisdom to know how to cherish that happiness, and the courage to believe you deserve it."

Niamh's eyes filled, and she battled tears.

Nora nodded, as though understanding the surfeit of emotions, squeezed Niamh's arms, and moved to join the celebrating O'Rourkes.

Cormac wrapped an arm around her waist, tugging her to his side. "What did she say to upset you?" he asked, as he kissed her head.

"Nothing," she breathed, as she pressed her face into his strong chest. "She gave me a blessing. I hope I am strong enough to live up to it."

CHAPTER 11

A heavy snow had fallen, and Cormac looked out his window to see his fiancée, niece, and soon-to-be sister-in-law outside. "What are they doing?" After donning a coat, hat, scarf, and gloves, he slipped outside to join them.

At the sound of his door closing, Niamh spun around and glared at him, her hands on her hips. "You've ruined our surprise!"

He pointed at his cabin with a thumb. "Should I go back inside and act like I didn't see you?"

Maggie gave a huff as she knelt on the ground. "No, because I think we'll need your strength. We wanted to build you a snowman, but the snow is so heavy!"

Cormac smiled at Maggie's enthusiasm and at Niamh's desire to do such a sweet surprise for him. "I'm an excellent beast of burden."

After they had made three snowmen, numerous snow angels, and had an impromptu snowball fight, Niamh said, "I'm freezing. I need to warm up."

"Me too," Maggie said, "and I'm sure Maura needs a nap. Why don't I take her back so you and Cormac can drink tea by his fire?" She winked at them, scooped up a giggling Maura, and trotted toward home.

Niamh sat, in quiet shock, covered head to foot in snow, panting from the exertion of the snowball fight, as she watched her daughter happily depart with her giggling sister. "Brazen," she whispered.

"Not brazen, love," Cormac said, as he groaned while heaving her to her feet. "Thoughtful. She's gifting us with time together. Which we haven't had nearly enough of since we became engaged a few weeks ago." He gripped her hand and pulled her toward his cabin.

Once inside, he shucked his outerwear, hanging it on pegs near the stove. He urged her to do the same.

"'Tis no use," she whispered. "I'm soaked through. I should go home."

He stilled her frenetic motions, whispering, "No, love." After kissing the riotous mass of her hair, come loose from all its pins during their exertions outside, he moved to a trunk and extracted a large nightshirt. "Change into this and cuddle with me under the blankets."

She gazed at him, wide-eyed and shocked.

"I promise I won't tempt you."

"You tempt me by breathing," she muttered.

"Niamh?" he rasped. "Say that again. Please." His gaze, filled with hope and yearning, met hers.

In a stronger voice, she said, "You tempt me by breathing, Cormac."

He pulled her into his embrace, wrapping his arms around her. "Good. As long as I don't frighten you. That is my greatest fear."

"No, I'm not afraid of you. Although I do fear what I feel for you," she whispered. When he would have said more, she shushed him and urged him to look the other way.

Cormac faced the stove, warming his front, as he attempted to battle his desire for Niamh, whom he would soon hold in his arms in his bed. He also attempted to fight his growing hope she felt the same depth of love for him as he did for her. Although he promised himself he would never force her into an admission, as such an avowal could never be construed as a true sentiment, he prayed every day for her to tell him how she felt. For him to know, with utter certainty, that she loved him.

"I'm decent," she called out.

"It's your turn now. Don't look," he said, before turning his head with a wicked smile and teasing glint in his eyes. "Unless you want to." At her mortified shriek, she tugged the blanket over her head.

After shucking all his soaked clothes, he tugged on another nightshirt and slipped under the covers with her.

"How is it that I'm so cold and you're a furnace?" she grumbled, as she instinctively moved into his embrace.

"You make it sound like all you desire me for is my warmth," he teased.

She snuggled into him and breathed a sigh of contentment. "You know that's not true, Cormac." She wrapped her arm around his belly, pressing into him.

After long moments of peaceful silence, broken only by the sounds of children playing outside and the crackling of wood in the fire, Cormac whispered, "What's the matter, love?"

She sighed. "I should have known better than to try to hide how I'm feeling from you. You've always known how to read me better than anyone." At his soft kiss to her temple, she relaxed. "I can't help but feel a tremendous guilt that we stole the happiness he should have had."

Cormac grunted and moved down so that his head was on the pillow, and he looked directly into her gaze. "Finally we'll talk about what happened." He saw her instinctual desire to withdraw into herself, but then she nodded. "Why did you never tell me what was occurring?"

Niamh shrugged. "Shame." She closed her eyes. When he stroked a whisper-soft caress over her cheeks, her eyes flared open in shock. "Every time he hit me, he had a reason. I didn't do something he wanted, and he felt compelled to punish me."

With shaking hands, Cormac held her head reverently. "You know that's a lie, my precious Niamh. Please say that you understand that he said those things to control you and to justify his abominable behavior to himself."

"On one level, I know that, Cormac," she whispered. "On another, I never believed I deserved better."

"Oh, my beloved," he breathed, leaning forward to kiss her softly on her forehead, then her nose, before finally kissing her lips. "You deserve the world. The stars and the moon, if you so wish. Never doubt."

Her eyes filled. "I did. Until recently. Until you." She raised a tremulous, hesitant hand to his face. "I thought … I thought if you knew how I had allowed him to treat me that you'd no longer respect me. That you'd see me as the weak woman I am." She held fingers over his lips so she could continue to speak her deepest truths.

"I feared, if you saw who I really was, a terrified woman living in a hell I'd made for myself, that you would no longer come by the house. You'd no longer brighten my days with your presence." She paused. "No longer give me hope that you would visit," she whispered. "And I found I couldn't live without hope."

He rested his forehead against hers. "I hate imagining the pain you suffered." He fought a shudder. "And I can't stand that it was my brother who harmed you, Niamh." He leaned forward, kissing her softly. "I know you struggle with the same guilt I feel that Connor left in anger after seeing us together and then died."

She nodded, her eyes wide.

"I would apologize, but I can't," he whispered, his voice tormented as his hands stroked through her tangled hair. "I can't because it was the first time I held you in my arms and you thought of me. You wanted me."

Her gaze was filled with hope at his passionate words. "I did, Cormac," she whispered. "But it wasn't the first time I wanted you. It wasn't the first time I desired your touch." She took a deep breath, as though garnering her courage. "It was the first time I dared to dream that you and I could have more than fantasies."

Cormac stared into her eyes a long moment, his gaze clouded with uncertainty and confusion. "I don't understand why you waited so long. You knew how much you meant to me after Connor and I fought in August."

She flushed and ducked her head. "Connor had convinced me that you considered me your sister. That you only defended me out of familial duty. Not because you felt more for me." She met his gaze. "Then I heard Connor taunting you. Goading you with the fact that I was his wife and that, no matter how much you might want me, you'd never have me. I peered through a crack in the wood wall and saw your stricken face. In that moment, I realized I was more than a sister to you."

He swallowed, as though too mortified by the overheard conversation to do anything else. "He excelled at manipulation."

Niamh nodded. "Aye, an' I decided, in that moment, I'd had enough. I'd suffered enough. I wanted more." She closed her eyes. "And, may God forgive me, my prayers were answered."

Cormac eased a tense Niamh onto his chest. "What do you mean?"

One hand played with his fingers, and she rested her head on his shoulder. "I had prayed, every night for over a year, for Connor to die."

Cormac chuckled and shook his head. "No matter what you believe, love, you don't have that power." He sighed. "I've thought a lot since I returned from Virginia City. I'll always feel guilty that Connor died. That we fought before he stormed away. That he said horrible things to us. But you didn't kill him any more than I did. His choices led to his death."

Niamh wrapped her arm around Cormac's waist and squeezed him tight, earning a stuttering sound of surprise and relief from him. "I know, Cormac, but sometimes guilt is easier to feel than relief and gratitude."

"Cormac, see sense," Niamh snapped, one hand on her waist. She glared up at him as he glowered down at her. They stood in the middle of his small cabin, searching for a place for Maura to sleep.

"There's no room for her here. And I won't feel comfortable if she's in the same room with us."

He stared at her intently for a long moment. "You're saying you won't feel comfortable making love with me if your daughter is here."

She nodded and flushed, facing away from him, as though searching the room for a hidden door to a second room to be made into a bedroom. "This is a perfect space for a single bachelor. Not for a man with a family."

Cormac crossed his arms over his chest. "No. I will not do it, and you shouldn't want to either, Niamh."

"It's the most logical step, Cormac." She held her hand up in the air and then dropped it down, slapping it against her thigh in agitation. "It's just sitting there, vacant, getting dusty."

"Aye, dusty because anyone with sense knows better than to enter it," he hissed. "That was the home of your abuse, Niamh. How can we start our new future together there, when the past will haunt us at every moment?" He waited for her to say something, but she stared at him as though he were being so unreasonable, there was nothing more to say. "Every time you reach for a bowl, wash dishes, go to bed, or turn to the door, you will think of him. Not me. Never of me." He shook his head, incredulous. "How can you expect me to live like that?"

"How can you expect me to live in this shack?" she yelled and then paled.

"It isn't a shack," he said in a low voice. "It's more finely wrought than the place you called home for years. It doesn't leak in winter and manages to remain cool in summer. The stove is of a higher quality than anything Connor bought you." When she shook her head and stared at him in exasperation, he broke off with his examples, making his home superior to the one she'd shared with his brother.

"There isn't enough room," she enunciated, as though she were speaking with someone who didn't speak English. "I will never be comfortable living here."

He leaned over, his eyes filled with rage as a panic filled him. "I'm not your father. I won't build you a small palace, Niamh. I'm a simple man, doin' the best I can."

She sighed and closed her eyes, her rage seeping away. "Oh, Cormac, I know you are. I don't want you to be different than you are. But I do want a home large enough for us to live in." She flushed as she gripped his hand. "I want a place for us to have privacy. Can't you understand that?"

He sighed and swore, stomping away from her as he paced the small confines of his home. "Fine. For now, we will live there. But not for long. Only until I think of a better solution." He spun just in time to catch her as she threw herself at him. "You won't win every argument, love," he murmured, as he kissed her head.

"No, but I know you'll listen to me and will consider my point of view. That's priceless, Cormac." She stood on her toes to kiss his jaw before she backed away. "I have to meet Mum and Maggie. We're goin' to clean the house and prepare it for after the wedding."

He gripped her hands, raising each one to kiss as he stared into her eyes. "Remember. I want a simple ceremony, lass. I don't need anything fancy, as long as you are walking down the aisle."

"Good, because simple is all you can manage in December in Fort Benton." She giggled as he kissed her again, racing away to meet her mother and sister.

Cormac ran a hand through his hair, afraid he'd just agreed to the first mistake of his marriage.

The day before his marriage to Niamh, Cormac evaded his friends and soon-to-be brothers-in-law and their attempts at a party for him. He had no desire to mourn the loss of his impending freedom. He relished the fact he would soon marry Niamh, binding the two of them together forever. His greatest fear was that she would come to realize this was a mistake and would stand him up at the altar tomorrow.

He shivered as he walked away from the town, up a small knoll and to an area with a rickety fence. Inside were the graves of the few who had perished upon their arrival at Fort Benton. Glancing at the scattered graves, he wondered at the lost hopes, the unfulfilled dreams of those who had perished too soon. Unerringly, his gaze landed on that of his brother's.

With resolute steps, he approached Connor's grave. Rather than cry or fall to his knees in sorrow, he stood in front of it with tense shoulders and fisted hands. "Connor," he rasped. His jaw clenched with anger, and he shook his head, as though in disbelief. "I never thought I could feel more rage than I did in August. But then I always did underestimate you."

After taking a stuttering breath, he said in a low, unfaltering voice, "I marry Niamh tomorrow. I will show her what it is to be esteemed above all others. To know what it is to have the respect and admiration of the one who has promised to honor and cherish you." He kicked at the snow near the grave. "I will show her that vows are not empty words. That there are men who fulfill their promises."

He stood here for long minutes, as though waiting to hear a response from Connor. Instead, the wind continued its susurrus symphony over the snow-dappled ground.

Cormac closed his eyes and unfisted his hands. He took a deep breath, relaxing his shoulders. "I don't know what mischief you intended with your will. But you did not succeed, Connor. Niamh and I will be together. Maura will never be separated from those who love her. And you will only be remembered as the man who had everything but wasn't wise enough to value the treasure he held within his hands."

CHAPTER 12

On a bright, cold morning in early December, Cormac paced his small cabin. He knew he needed to head to the O'Rourkes' house soon, but he wanted a few moments alone before joining the boisterous family for his wedding to Niamh. He paused in his pacing, as he envisioned her walking toward him, her smile serene and her eyes lit with delight and hope. He fingered the simple silver ring in his waistcoat pocket, praying he wouldn't lose it before it was time to give it to her. "I hope it's good enough for her," he whispered aloud.

He ran a hand over his suit and then over his head. He'd tied back his long hair, although it wasn't as long as usual. He'd had the barber trim it the previous day. Although he'd considered shaving off his beard, he'd had that trimmed too. Now he looked less like a wild woodsman and more like an urbane businessman. He chuckled as he held up his hands. If his calluses were ignored.

At the noise at his front door, he called out, "What?" He sighed as he saw Kevin and Ardan O'Rourke on his steps. "Were you afraid I wouldn't come? I'm not that much of a fool."

"No," Kevin said, as he slapped Cormac on the shoulder and pushed him back, as he and Ardan forced their way inside. "No, we know you won't miss your chance to marry Niamh. But 'tis tradition for the groom to be heckled by a family member."

Ardan held his arms wide. "Thus, here we are."

Kevin nodded with a wink. "Aye." He looked Cormac over and smirked. "The shave and haircut don't make you any less wild, Cormac."

Cormac lifted a self-conscious hand to his face and scrubbed over it, his shoulders stooping with momentary disappointment. "Really? I thought it was an improvement."

Ardan laughed. "Niamh liked you just fine when you looked like a half-tamed wild man. There's no need to change for her."

Shrugging, Cormac said, "Well, I know she's making an effort for the wedding. I thought I should too."

Kevin smiled. "You should see the cake Deirdre made you. I know she's a wonderful cook and can feed the men hearty fare, but she should be a baker." He sighed with pleasure. "I can't wait to eat my fill of it."

"Glutton," Ardan said, as he tapped his brother on his stomach. "An' I can attest it tastes better than it looks. She made a small test cake, and we ate that for dinner last night."

Cormac chuckled. "So that's why you weren't at the prewedding dinner. You were too busy feasting on my cake."

Ardan shrugged. "Deirdre adores Niamh and wanted her wedding gift to be perfect."

Cormac paled and stared at the two brothers in horror. "A wedding gift. I don't have a wedding gift for my bride."

Rolling his eyes, Kevin said, "You mean, beside your heart, your home, and your honor?" Clapping a hand on Cormac's shoulder, he said, "Never fear. Niamh won't want for anything else."

Relaxing slightly, Cormac allowed the O'Rourke brothers to lead him from his cabin to their parents' home, where his bride and his future awaited him.

～

Niamh stood, staring at her reflection, fighting fear that she was repeating history in having faith in another man, as she waited with nervous anticipation on her wedding day. Her fingers traced over the beautiful robin's-egg blue dress Aileen had sewn for her.

Maggie slipped into the room, dressed in a wool evergreen dress with her blue eyes lit with delight. She frowned as she stared at her sister. "What's the matter, Niamh?" When her sister failed to respond, she fisted a hand on her hip and tapped her foot on the floor. "Do you wish me to leave? Do you wish someone else was here with you now?"

Just as Maggie was about to storm from the room, Niamh grabbed her sister's arm and shook her head. "No, Maggie, no," she whispered. "I'm woolgathering." She flushed. "I'm trying to gather my courage."

Her frown intensifying, Maggie walked farther into the room to perch on one of the chairs. "Why would you need any courage to marry Cormac?" She shrugged. "I know they say Connor deserved everything he had coming to him, so why would you mourn him today?"

"I don't mourn him, Maggie," Niamh hissed, her eyes flashing with irritation. She took a deep breath and rolled her shoulders, as she attempted to relax. "I worry I'm entering into the same sort of hell I knew." She looked at her sister. "Imagine what living with Jacques would have been like. That was what my life with Connor was like." She closed her eyes in defeat when she saw Maggie pale.

"Oh, Niamh, that's a misery past bearing." She closed her eyes for a moment. "I thought he was a fool to go to the Bordello, for how could any man want a Siren when he could have you, but ..."

Niamh let out a small appreciative laugh and moved to sit beside her sister. "Oh, Maggie, how can you be so loyal, so good, to someone who's never treated you well?" When her sister stared at her with a blank expression, Niamh spoke in a halting low voice, "I've resented you from the moment you returned. And I'm sorry."

"You liked being the only sister. The only daughter." Maggie shrugged. "Why would you want to have that role usurped?"

"No," Niamh said, as she shook her head and grasped Maggie's hand. "That's not it at all. Do you know how many times, when we were struggling in the years Da was married to Colleen, that I prayed for a sister? That I wished for someone who could understand what I was going through?" A tear coursed down her cheek. "We have wonderful brothers, aye, but they don't have a clue what it means to be a young woman. To go through the changes we do." She flushed. "An' they have no interest in discussing topics other than politics or work or sports."

"You were lonely," Maggie breathed, her gaze filled with dawning understanding and wonder.

"Desperately." After taking another deep breath, Niamh admitted, "And then you returned. And you'd had Mum all that time. The mum I had so desperately needed. The envy about drove me mad."

"Oh, Niamh," Maggie whispered and then giggled. "I was jealous of you having Da. Instead I had Francois, then Jacques."

They leaned into each other, wrapping arms around each other in a sideways hug. "I'm so glad you returned to us," Niamh whispered after many minutes.

"Me too," Maggie said. Taking a deep breath, "And, as I am your sister, I have the right to give you sisterly advice." She met Niamh's amused stare and giggled once before sobering. "Trust in Cormac. He's a good man." She bit her lip. "He stares at you the way Dunmore stares at me, and that can only be a good thing."

Niamh gaped at her. "You know about Dunmore?"

Maggie flushed. "It's hard not to notice."

"If he makes you uncomfortable, I'll ask Da to cease inviting him to family functions," Niamh said, her hand gripping Maggie's.

"No!" She bit her lip. "No. He's like a brother. Sort of." Her gaze was filled with confusion, when she met Niamh's. "I don't know what he is, but I don't dislike him." She shook her head. "But my point is, a man who stares at you like that, like you alone were the reason the sun rose, won't hurt you, Niamh." She kissed her sister on her cheek and hopped up. "I have to help Mum."

Niamh watched her leave, her mind whirling from her conversation with Maggie.

Niamh stood in the hallway leading into the living room, listening to the rumble of voices. If she focused, she knew she could make out conversations. However, she preferred to allow the cacophony of voices to wash over her, as she smoothed a hand over her skirts—hoping to as easily calm her nerves. Although she had professed her trust in Cormac, she found that marrying him required a leap of faith she had never thought to make again.

Closing her eyes, she attempted to banish images from her first wedding day. Of Connor glancing over his shoulder as she walked toward him and the triumphant gleam in his eye, as though he had just won a bet. Of Cormac, standing sullenly beside him, his gaze guarded and more remote with each step she took toward Connor. Of the perfunctory kiss bestowed by Connor and his eager desire for approval and acceptance from Seamus. From the moment she said "I do," she had suspected Connor had only seen her as a means to an end. As a way to earn entry into the O'Rourke business and to access the O'Rourke funds.

"Niamh," Seamus whispered, interrupting her reverie. "'Tis time, love," he whispered.

Pasting on a smile, Niamh slipped her hand through her da's arm.

"Take a deep breath, love, and imagine Cormac waiting for you," he murmured. "Imagine the love and hope shining in his eyes. Forget your past disappointments." He paused until he felt her relax beside him. "Good girl."

"Thank you, Da," she whispered, as she squeezed his arm.

"Anything for you, my darling daughter," he said, as they slowly walked into the room. Niall played a gentle song on his fiddle, his green eyes shining with pride to have had such an important task entrusted to him.

Niamh looked ahead, her gaze entranced by the sight of Cormac waiting for her with Maura in his arms. He had tied back his hair and had trimmed his beard, but her focus was on the love and promise of joy in his gaze. She fought the urge to run to him and smiled as Da chuckled, as though he understood her desire.

Soon she stood in front of Cormac, with a priest Dunmore had brought back with him on his last-ditch trek through the Territory before winter struck.

"Hello, beautiful," Cormac said to Niamh, smiling as Maura patted at his face. "Yes, you're my beauty too," he said to his niece. With a hopeful smile, he said to Niamh, "I wanted you to understand that I am sincere in caring for both of you. In marrying you, I want to be husband and father." His gaze pleaded with her to understand.

"Thank you, Cormac," she whispered. "Nothing could have touched me more."

He raised her hand, kissing her fingers, before they turned to face the priest, who watched them with avid interest. When Maura became fussy, Mary took her.

Niamh clasped Cormac's hand throughout the ceremony, her voice loud and strong as she said her vows.

When the priest said, "You may kiss the bride," Niamh turned to Cormac with a wary expression. However, he continued to look as though he were the most fortunate man, his gaze glowing with wonder.

He cupped her face and slowly lowered his head to hers, whispering, "Don't be afraid, my beloved. We're wed, as we always should have been." He kissed her, a slow, passionate kiss before backing away, as her family cheered.

Niamh blushed, leaning into his side. When Maura toddled to them, Niamh took one of her daughter's hands, while Cormac clasped her other, and they walked down the small aisle with Maura between them. As Niamh saw her family congratulating Cormac, she saw no cunning in his gaze. All she beheld was a tremendous relief and pride that she had finally agreed to be his.

~

Cormac led Niamh outside, after they had eaten their fill of the fine food and the decadent cake. He'd tried to drink as little as possible of Seamus's whiskey, although he'd still drunk more than he wanted to, as each of Niamh's eldest brothers had raised a toast in Cormac's honor. "Come, love," he murmured, as he grasped her hand and guided her through the path to his small cabin.

"Cormac, this isn't where we are supposed to go," she whispered, as she fought a shiver.

"Yes, it is," he argued, kicking open the door and then swinging her into his arms, earning a startled shriek from her. He marched inside, slamming the door shut behind him and gazed deeply into her eyes. "We might live in his house, but I'll be damned if I spend my wedding night there."

"I wish you could understand that all that matters is that we are together," she whispered, her fingers tracing over his cheeks. "My handsome husband," she whispered. "I never thought to see you with a trimmed beard."

He smiled, kissing the palm of her hand. "There is little I wouldn't do for you, Niamh, and I wanted to please you today."

She smiled shyly at him. "You pleased me by showing up." She flushed as he chuckled at her honesty. She frowned as she stared into his gaze. "Are you well, Cormac?"

He groaned, sitting on the bed with her on his lap. "I drank more whiskey than I wanted to." He kissed her head as she giggled. "But I didn't know how to avoid it with each toast."

"You do realize some brothers gave us three toasts," she said with a wry smile. "They wanted to see if you'd catch on."

Groaning, Connor flopped to his back, his hand on her waist to keep her steady. She still shrieked as she toppled to the side and landed beside him. "Give me a moment, love, and I'll be fine." His hand reached out to intertwine with hers. "Do you know what I felt when I saw you in this beautiful dress, walking toward me?" he whispered, his gaze filled with love and pride. "Peace that finally we were to marry. That nothing would keep us apart ever again."

She smiled as she cupped his face, tilted toward hers. "Do you know what I felt when I saw you holding Maura?" At his shake of his head, she beamed at him, as a tear of joy trickled down her cheek. "Absolute wonder that you knew how much I wanted her to be a part of the ceremony."

"I love her too," he whispered. "I could see the delight in your gaze." He kissed her hand, still cupping his cheek. "And I was so eager to become your husband."

"Yes," she murmured. "The absolute joy I felt knowing I would be your wife." Her grin faded as she saw his eyes fluttering as he battled sleep. "Cormac?" she whispered. In answer, a soft snore sounded.

She sat up in her wedding finery, as her husband rested crossways on the bed. "Oh, what am I to do with you?" she whispered. She bit her lip because she knew she couldn't ask her brothers for help. They would never cease teasing them if they knew Cormac fell asleep on her on their wedding night. Thus, she eased off a boot, and then the other, hoping her struggle would wake him up. Instead, he seemed to be more comfortable, and he curled onto his side.

Rising, Niamh wandered to a trunk and flipped it open. Inside, she found heavy blankets. After tossing one over him, she pulled one out for herself and sat in a chair in front of the fire. With a rueful smile, she admitted to herself that her nerves about her second wedding night had been completely unfounded.

~

Waking in fits and starts, Cormac shivered and stretched. He swallowed and tried to pry his eyes open but felt as though he had walked on the prairie for days. Shivering and then moaning, he pushed and pulled at the blanket, uncertain if he wanted it to cover him or not.

"Cormac," Niamh whispered. "Drink this and you'll start to feel better."

He sniffed, smelling coffee, and he allowed her to ease him up.

After taking a swig of the lukewarm drink, he set the mug aside and peered at her with a bleary gaze. "Niamh, love, why are you here?"

She chuckled. "We married yesterday, Cormac. Or don't you remember?"

With a groan, he bowed his head and sighed with pleasure. "Yes. You wore a beautiful dress, and your hair shone like a shimmering sunset." He frowned as he leaned up on his elbows, his expression filled with pain. "I don't remember easing you from your gown." His gaze took in her serviceable green woolen dress.

She shrugged. "You didn't. You fell asleep a few moments after arriving here."

Groaning, he ran a hand over his face. "God, forgive me, Niamh. I never meant to be such a disappointment."

She laughed and took his hand. "No, you delight me," she whispered. "The fact that the toasts and the meager amount of whiskey affected you …" She shrugged.

"You're delighted I can't handle my liquor better?" he asked, as though she had just handed him the greatest insult.

"Aye," she said, as she beamed at him. "Connor could have drunk all my brothers and father under the table and then done it again. 'Tis a relief to see how different you are from him."

Groaning again, Cormac tugged on Niamh's hand, until she fell forward and rested in his arms. "I never took to drink like he did." He breathed in deeply of her subtle scent, sighing with pleasure at the feel of her beside him. "I've always hated feeling like this." Kissing her head, he murmured, "There's too much to do to be bogged down with a frequent hangover."

"'Tis because you are a good man, Cormac. An' determined to provide well for us." She raised their joined hands and kissed his.

With a muttered curse, he whispered, "I dreamed of a night of passion between us, Niamh, before we moved into his home. Not a night where you listened to me snore." He grumbled as she giggled at his accurate assessment of how she'd passed the evening.

"We'll have our passion, Cormac." She paused and bit her lip. "But not yet. I still need a little time."

141

With a sigh, he rested his forearm over his face. "I'm a fool to have missed my chance with you."

"You didn't miss it." She kissed his arm and then his cheek. "You postponed it, *a shíorghrá.* Nothing more."

CHAPTER 13

A howling wind blew, threatening more snow, and Cormac pulled his fleece-lined jacket tighter around him. He had lost his scarf, and his oxen had trampled his knit hat, so he huddled in the cold outside the O'Rourke warehouse. Cormac knocked on the door again, cursing the fierce wind, as he feared it would prevent anyone inside from hearing him. After his third knock went unanswered, he tried the door and eased it open. "Hello?" he called out.

"Yes?" Seamus O'Rourke answered from a side room Cormac knew was his office.

"It's Cormac." He stood in the large room, staring at the nearly empty shelves. "Hello, sir," he said, with a deferential nod to Seamus. "Seems you ordered well last year and sold out of most of your supplies."

"Aye, we had a good year." He shrugged, as though a thriving business was not all that important. "Mary an' Maggie were returned to us. Niamh's happy again. That is what made the year tremendous." He tilted his head to the side to study the younger man. "I have a sense that's not what brought you by."

Cormac chuckled. "Astute as always, Mr. O'Rourke."

"*Seamus*, lad. We're family." He stilled as he saw the restless unease thrumming through Cormac. "How'd you know to come here rather than the big house?"

Shrugging, Cormac moved to the small stove in Seamus's office to warm up. "I saw the light and thought I'd try here." He stared at the stove, as though in a trance. He jolted when Seamus clapped him on his shoulder and pushed him to a chair near the stove.

"Sit. Tell me what's botherin' you, lad."

Cormac paused, his mind a jumble of questions and competing loyalties. "It's more a desire to understand, sir," he said in a low voice. "Niamh and I have been married a few weeks. But little has improved." He closed his eyes, as though he'd imparted too much. "I beg your pardon, sir."

"You think I don't know my daughter grows more prickly than a hedgehog as the days pass?" Seamus sighed. "We all see it, lad."

"I don't know what to do," he whispered, ducking his head with the shame of admitting his inability to keep his wife happy.

"Do you truly want my advice?" At Cormac's nod, Seamus leaned forward with his elbows on his knees. His blue eyes shone with sincerity as he beheld his son-in-law. "Burn down the house you're livin' in. Too many memories are there, none of them good for my daughter. Move back to your wee cabin. You'll make do."

Cormac jerked at Seamus's blunt words and then nodded. "Yes, that house must be demolished." He gazed at Seamus inquisitively for a moment. "But perhaps not burned."

Seamus flushed and nodded. "The second thing 'tis not easy for a father to speak of." He closed his eyes and firmed his shoulders before blurting out, "Take my daughter to bed. Rid her of the doubts festerin' inside her."

"Sir," Cormac gasped, as he flushed as red as the fiery wood inside the stove. "I don't want to rush her."

"You call this rushin'?" Seamus chuckled. "You've been married a few weeks, an' you do little more than kiss her on the top of her head. How do you think that makes her feel, lad?" He waited as Cormac covered his face with his palms, as though mortified to have such a conversation with his father-in-law.

"How did you do it?" he whispered. At Seamus's perplexed look, Cormac asked, "How did you help Mary past her fears and doubts and prove your love?"

Seamus closed his eyes, as though suffering a body blow. "Ah, lad." He sighed as he relaxed into the chair. After a long moment spent contemplating the stove, he murmured, "Mary an' I had a history too, aye? But it was one of love and passion, which you never had with Niamh. You had longing and hope and disillusionment." His eyes shone with remorse as he stared at Cormac. "And, aye, I had disillusionment too. And fear. Fear she'd never overcome her time with Francois."

Seamus paused, as he took a deep breath and then expelled it. "But then I had my own fears. I'd failed my second wife. What if I'd changed since I was with Mary and couldn't be the man she needed me to be?" He shared a terror-filled gaze with Cormac.

"But you *were* the man she needed," Cormac argued.

"Aye, I was. I was patient and constant in my love." He paused, as though remembering a not-too-distant scene with his wife. "And I listened when she reassured me that she needed more from me than a brotherly embrace." Seamus battled embarrassment and faced his son-in-law. "Face your fears, Cormac, so you can help Niamh through hers."

"Damn," Cormac rasped, as he dropped his head into his hands. The wood crackled and popped in the stove for many minutes. Finally Cormac spoke again. "All this time, I've allowed her to cloak herself in her fears, afraid I would never be the man she truly needs." He paused. "I've allowed Connor to keep us apart."

Seamus reached out and gripped Cormac's shoulder. "He'll always be with the two of you. He played an indelible role in your lives, aye?" When Cormac nodded and rubbed at his eyes, Seamus paused. "What more is it, lad?"

Cormac rose, pacing to the far end of the small office and then back again. "He was my brother, and all I feel is anger. And such hatred." He ducked his head. "And I'm so ashamed."

"Why, Cormac? You didn't harm Niamh. You've cherished her since the day you met her."

The younger man turned away to stare at the evening-blackened world outside, as though looking for a lodestar. "I didn't stop it," he whispered. "I suspected, and feared, what was occurring, and did nothing. And that is my greatest shame." He ducked his head as he gripped the windowsill.

For long minutes, the office was silent. So silent, Cormac feared Seamus had slipped out on soundless feet, so disgusted with him that he couldn't bear to spend another moment in his presence. With an aching heart, he turned to return to Connor's home, stilling when he saw Seamus, staring at him with an infinite amount of patience. "Sir," he gasped in surprise.

Seamus rose, his eyes squinting to see Cormac stiffen, as though awaiting a blow. Slowly he raised his arms to rest his hands on the younger man's shoulders. "You failed her, Cormac. And that is your burden to bear." Seamus clamped his jaw shut a moment before he choked out, "An' 'tis mine as well. As it is her brothers. We all suspected but couldn't bear for it to be true."

"I don't understand, sir," Cormac whispered.

"Do you wonder at the distance that existed between Maggie and Niamh before your weddin'?"

Cormac watched him with confusion.

Seamus shrugged in a self-deprecating manner. "Maggie returns, while bein' threatened by a man the likes of Jacques Bergeron. Her brothers an' I vow we will do everythin' in our powers to protect the wee creature. Vow she'll never suffer again. An', all the while, we ignore poor Niamh and all she was sufferin'."

"You're being too harsh, Seamus."

"Perhaps, but I hate that I didn't see what was right before me. I couldn't bear the thought I had allowed my daughter to marry a brutal man, never mind a lazy, worthless one." He flushed but did not take back his words, even though they were said against Cormac's brother.

"How do you think I feel? He was my brother," Cormac whispered.

Seamus moved to lean against his desk. "Explain somethin' I don't understand. What happened to make Connor go to the Bordello that night?"

Cormac flushed and shook his head.

"'Tis shameful?"

"No," Cormac said, with an emphatic shake of his head. "Not for me. I fear it is for Niamh." He closed his eyes. "She believes we caused Connor's death."

"How?" Seamus asked, as he crossed his arms over his chest, his brows furrowed, as he attempted and failed to puzzle out Cormac's words from what he knew about the night Connor died. "He drank too much, lost at cards, and went to the Bordello, lookin' for someone other than his wife to beat. What more is there to know?"

Cormac closed his eyes and massaged the back of his neck. "Ah," he murmured and cleared his throat. "There's the small matter of him finding Niamh kissing me. In their kitchen."

"Oh, lad," Seamus whispered. "I'm surprised he didn't kill you." He paled. "Or Niamh."

Cormac's eyes gleamed with righteous anger. "He promised her that he'd 'take care of her' when he got home. I warned him, if he ever touched Niamh again, I'd kill him. That I'd never consider him family if he continued to harm his wife." He closed his eyes, as though reliving the argument. "We said horrible, unforgiveable things to each other. And then he died."

A yawning smile spread, and Seamus gave a small *whoop*. At Cormac's perplexed look, Seamus gripped his shoulder. "Don't you see, lad? You *did* defend Niamh. When she needed you most, you were there."

"I beg your pardon, sir, but you have faulty logic. If I hadn't been caught kissing my brother's wife, I wouldn't have needed to defend her."

Shaking his head, Seamus continued to beam at him. "No, no matter what he saw, Connor would have found a reason to lash out at Niamh. Think, lad. When does Niamh shy away from you?"

"Whenever she fears I'll strike out," Cormac whispered. He shared a tormented stare with Seamus. "Which is all too frequent."

147

"Aye, which means Connor always looked for an excuse to hand out a punishment. Men like that refuse to be responsible for their actions, Cormac. They like to believe others have pushed them to do what they had to do." He sobered. "For Mary, 'twas because the dinner was late. Or she didn't smile readily enough. Or she called her daughter *Maggie*, rather than *Margaret*."

"Utter nonsense," Cormac sputtered.

"Aye, to men with honor, aye. To weak men, looking for a reason to feel superior, they were justifiable reasons to warrant their abuse." Seamus looked around the office, as though noting the late hour. "Come. 'Tis time for supper. An' time for you to woo your wife."

Cormac stilled at Seamus's departure. "Will you and Mary watch Maura?" At Seamus's nod, Cormac smiled. "I have one last thing to ask of you."

Niamh let out a huff of annoyance as she stood on the steps of Cormac's cabin. She knocked on the door, listening for his footsteps as they approached. Somehow she could tell they were his and not Connor's. Rather than an impatient pounding as Connor stormed to the door, as he stormed through life, the slow cadence of Cormac's walk reminded her of a lilting dance. "Fool," she muttered to herself for her fanciful thoughts, as she shivered again in the cold. She whispered the single word to herself again as the door burst open to reveal her handsome husband. Her husband who still didn't want her.

"Niamh," he breathed, his blue eyes lit with delight. "You came."

"Da made it sound urgent," she said, as she brushed past him into the warmth of his cabin. She moved to the stove to warm her feet and hands. "Why are you here and not at home?" She shivered as she felt him along her back, his nimble fingers playing with the pins in her hair. When his breath teased at her nape, she gasped and arched back into him.

"That isn't our home, Niamh. I was a fool to be convinced to live there." He whispered in her ear, "I'm tired of living with a ghost." He reached around the front of her, releasing the clasp of her cloak and easing it off her. He backed up just enough to allow it to pool at her feet before he stepped forward again, his warmth as captivating as any heat emanating from the stove. "Aren't you?"

"What?" she gasped, as she arched into his light touch down the front of her dress and then back up again. She tilted her head to one side, as he gave her breathy kisses along her neck. "Cormac," she moaned.

"What?" he asked in an innocent tone. "My wife is cold, and I wanted to warm her."

"Please, warm me some more," she whispered. "I …" Her shoulders tensed for a moment, until she felt soft kisses along her shoulder blades. "My dress is damp and should be removed."

"Excellent idea," he said, humor lacing his voice. "I'd hate for my beloved to catch a chill." His adroit hands released the buttons along the front of her dress, allowing him to give her a full-body hug as he remained behind her. His large body held her cocooned in his warm and loving embrace, while his mouth planted soft kisses alongside her neck.

His fingers, always skilled, seemed to slip easily to the side, gently caressing the curves of her breasts and then the softness of her belly, as he eased the buttons open. By the time he slipped the dress over her shoulders and to her hips, Niamh was panting and shivering with each touch.

"How is your corset, love?" he whispered.

"Soaked," she gasped.

"Wonderful," he teased.

Cormac repeated the same tortuous, loving caresses as he eased open the ties. Niamh's moans melded with his, as he continued to caress and to tantalize her with the passion smoldering between them. When she was free of the corset, Niamh took a deep breath as she fell backward into his arms. All that separated them now was her shift. Rather than a gentle kiss to her neck, he nipped the point her neck met her shoulder, pausing when she yelped. "Forgive me," he said, as he moved to step away. His arms dropped from her, ending his contact with her.

"No," she cried out. "No, please. I've never known such pleasure, Cormac. Don't stop. Don't tease me and then stop." She turned to face him, her hazel eyes glowing with passion. "Please, show me what we can have. Show me what it is to be treasured."

"You have always been treasured," he said, passion and love lighting his gaze.

"Never before now. Never until you," she whispered. "Please, *a shíorghrá.*"

"You never have to ask twice," he whispered, as he swooped down to capture her mouth in a rapturous kiss. "If there's ever anything you don't like, tell me. If you want to stop, tell me." He looked deeply into her eyes. "I'll never be angry with you, Niamh, for speaking your truth."

She smiled tremulously and cupped his cheek. "Make love with me, husband."

"With every pleasure," he rasped.

~

A fterward, they lay in a tangle in the sheets on his bed. *Our bed,* his mutinous mind insisted. He had no desire to ever return to his brother's home to see her eyes become shadowed as she was lost to another memory. He wanted to start anew here. With Maura. He closed his eyes as he considered the small cabin. There was barely room for the two of them, never mind what he hoped would be a growing family.

As he attempted to push away his concerns, his hands continued to stroke Niamh's soft skin as she rested on his chest. Her soft breaths stirred a tenderness inside him which he feared was boundless. Now that he truly felt like a husband, *Niamh's husband,* he feared there was nothing he wouldn't do to keep her safe. Or happy.

At her soft sigh, he kissed her forehead. "Are you awake?" he whispered.

"Yes," she murmured, as she snuggled closer. "I never want to leave this bed."

"Good," he said, as he fought puffing out his chest with masculine pride. "It means you were satisfied."

She lifted her head to rest her chin on his chest, so she could gaze into his beautiful eyes. Never before had they been so unguarded and so filled with happiness. Her hand rose for her fingers to play over his eyebrow and then to brush at his hair. "*Satisfied?* Is that what you call it?" She made a soothing sound when she felt him stiffen beneath her. She smiled mischievously at him, her gaze filled with playfulness. "I'd call it *rapture.*"

"*Rapture?*" he asked. His breath caught at the look in her eyes. A look he'd never seen before. The look of a well-loved woman, unashamed of the passion she felt. A woman confident of the man who held her in his arms.

"Perhaps *bliss* is a better word," she teased, as she kissed his chest and then leaned up to kiss the underside of his jaw, her soft lips scraping against his trimmed beard.

"*Bliss,*" he breathed.

"Or *ecstasy,*" she said, stifling a screech as he rolled them over, so he loomed over her.

He stared into her eyes, as though searching for any sign of fear or hesitancy. When all he saw was the unfettered delight she had described, he groaned and pulled her closer. When her arms wrapped around him without hesitation, he breathed a sigh of relief. "God, how I love you, Niamh," he whispered. "I'll always love you."

"Never stop," she breathed, as she melted into his loving embrace. "Never stop."

Cormac wandered in the direction of the livery, with the absent idea of checking on his oxen. He knew they were well tended, and he had no real need to visit the livery. However, he had spent enough time at home, mooning over his new wife, and he felt a need for some sort of activity. With snow threatening, he had no desire to go on a walk and become stranded as a squall blew in.

As he strolled past the hotel, he came to an abrupt halt as Uriah Chaffee stepped from inside, blocking his path. "Mr. Chaffee," he said in a deferential manner, although his gaze gleamed with warning.

"Mr. Ahern," Uriah said, as he tucked his hands into his fur-lined black wool coat. "It seems you were as foolish as your brother believed you to be." He chuckled.

Cormac closed his eyes for a moment, battling his desire to ignore the meddlesome lawyer and his curiosity to know more. "I don't understand," he said, cringing, as his curiosity won.

Uriah rocked back onto his heels, as though delighting in having won a battle of wills with Cormac. "Your brother told me, over a few glasses of subpar whiskey, that he believed there was little you wouldn't do to marry his wife." Uriah's gaze gleamed with contempt. "I'm surprised the sheriff didn't consider arresting you for murder, as your actions were as much to blame for his death as anyone's."

Taking a warning step toward the lawyer, Cormac paused, fisting his hands and then breathing deeply. "Connor was to blame. For every misfortune that befell him and for every missed opportunity to know joy. I am nothing like him."

Shrugging, Uriah watched him with a sly look in his gaze. "Perhaps. Although it would have been better for everyone involved if you had remained in Virginia City for the winter." He sighed as he looked around the deserted streets of Fort Benton. "Of if I hadn't been forced to leave that vibrant little town."

"I imagine escaping with your life should have been reward enough," Cormac snapped, although he studied the lawyer closely. "Tell me, Chaffee. I heard a rumor recently that you had hoped Seamus would have to leave too, to find a lawyer to help Niamh. Is that true?"

With a roll of his eyes, Uriah stared at Cormac. "The entire proceedings have been unorthodox. There should always have been another lawyer, although I understand one of such high a caliber as I am is hard to find." He preened as he puffed out his growing paunch.

Cormac frowned as he stared at Chaffee. "What would you have to gain to have both of us away at the same time? And Dunmore?"

Uriah shook his head, tapping Cormac on his shoulder. "The problem, dear boy, is that there are always O'Rourke men around. And there always will be. There are simply too many of them." He sauntered away, leaving Cormac deep in thought, as he resumed his walk to the livery.

When he arrived, he moved to the tack room to find Dunmore inside, reading a five-and-dime novel. "Dunmore," he said.

Dunmore flicked a glance in his direction but failed to greet him in any other way than to grunt "Hello," as he continued to read. He sat with his legs propped against the wall, two chair legs off the ground as he flipped pages. After a few minutes, he sighed, plopping the chair's front legs on the ground and glaring in Cormac's direction. "What's the matter? Your thinking is enough to drive me mad."

Cormac chuckled. "And your reading would drive anyone insane. I'd learn to quiet your *hmms* and *ohs* before courting wee Maggie." He laughed as Dunmore belted him with his book. He leaned against the wall, one leg crossed over the other. "I ran into Chaffee."

Dunmore shrugged, his blue-green eyes alert, even though he sat with a forced calm. "That would be enough to rile anyone."

"Answer me this, Dun. Why would that man want you, me, and Seamus out of town at the same time?" He nodded as Dunmore sat upright, any sense of disinterest gone. "What would he have to gain?"

"Damn," Dunmore whispered. "I'd hoped we would only be cursed with his presence this winter. I fear he will be with us for a longer duration." When Cormac stared at him in confusion, Dunmore said, "Chaffee. I doubt he'll leave. He's going to stay to continue to stir up trouble. And he has his eye on one of the O'Rourkes."

Cormac's jaw clenched. "He can leave Niamh well enough alone. She's suffered enough."

"No, not Niamh," Dunmore said, with a shake of his head. "Maggie." When Cormac gaped at him, he nodded. "I'd heard rumblings but thought them too fantastic to believe. But I think he's in cahoots with

Jacques. For some reason, he is willing to aid that man. But I don't know why."

"We must warn Seamus," Cormac said.

Dunmore motioned for Cormac to calm and then nodded. "We will. But after the holidays. You know how much the man loves the holidays, and this year will be even more special because he has Maggie and Mary back. After the New Year, we'll inform him of the potential for the new threat."

When Cormac began to protest, Dunmore shook his head. "There's no way Jacques can travel here in the middle of winter, trapper or no trapper. Besides, the man's growing fat and lazy. He'll want to remain in Virginia City, with good food and biddable women. We won't see him again until next summer, at the earliest. And, when we do, we'll be ready."

CHAPTER 14

Nearly a week after her visit to Cormac's cabin and a few short days before Christmas, Niamh returned to the home she had shared with Connor. The home she finally understood could never be her home with Cormac. They needed a fresh start, although she feared she would never be allowed to overcome her poor judgment in marrying Connor.

Stumbling into the bedroom, Niamh curled onto the bed, sobbing, her arms wrapped around her belly. A keening wail emerged, and her sobs intensified until her body shook. "Why?" she whispered to no one. "Why can't I be allowed to be happy?" When that only made her sadder, she buried her face in a pillow and prayed for a strength she feared she didn't have.

Soft hands stroked down her back, and she instinctively relaxed. She knew it was Cormac, soothing her, as she feared he never would again. Turning, she pulled him down to the bed. "I need you to hold me, Cormac. Please. I know I'll be alone soon, but now, … now I need you to hold me." She clutched him to her, shaking with her sobs that refused to abate.

After many minutes, her tears finally quieted, and she remained in his arms, hiccupping and stuttering out gasping breaths.

"You're all right, my love," he whispered. "You'll never be alone. I'll never leave you alone."

Although she wouldn't have thought it possible, more tears leaked out. She pressed her cheek to his chest, breathing deeply of his masculine scent mixed with a hint of sweat. "You will," she whispered. "When you hear my news, I know you will. And I will never blame you."

Cormac eased her away as he stared at her, unable to hide the terror in his gaze. "Niamh, what are you talking about?" He ran a hand over her head, tangling his fingers in her silky hair. "Why would I ever leave you?"

She pushed away and then held a hand, palm out, to keep him from reaching for her again. "No, Cormac. I can't say what I have to say if you're touching me." Her gaze was filled with pleading, as she saw the hurt in his gaze. "Please, let me try." She cleared her throat and then rose to sit in a chair beside the bed. She wrapped her arms around her waist again and stared at a distant spot on the floor.

"Niamh," Cormac said, in a gentle but firm tone. "Whatever you have to tell me, look me in the eyes."

She took a deep breath, firming her shoulders slightly, although she remained in a mostly hunched position. She finally met his gaze, and a few more tears leaked out.

He blanched at the devastation he saw in her gaze. "What could have happened this morning, my love? We were so happy when you left the cabin." He swallowed and whispered, "Weren't we?"

She reached a hand out, as though to soothe him. "We were, Cormac. I swear, we were." She closed her eyes a moment, as though reliving the wondrous night they had spent together. Maura had slept in the spare bed in Maggie's room at her parents' house, and she and Cormac had had another night. *A belated extended honeymoon night*, her mother had called it. "I'm so sorry," she whispered again.

"Tell me," he demanded. When she didn't flinch at his harsh command, he felt a small measure of pleasure that she continued to grow in self-confidence, in his love for her.

After another fortifying breath, she spoke in a halting voice. "You know what my life with Connor was like. Always waiting for the next blow. For the next time he said something cruel." She sniffled. "He had always ignored Maura, except during the first few months, when she had colic. But when she began to crawl and try to walk, he found her a nuisance." She took a deep breath. "He kicked her in August," she breathed.

"What?" Cormac asked, his blue eyes blazing with anger.

She nodded, her gaze locked to his. "I jumped in front of her, screaming like a madwoman." She closed her eyes a moment. "I said he could do what he liked with me but never to our daughter." She swallowed. "He took me at my word."

"That's when he beat you so terribly," Cormac breathed. After a long moment of silence, he asked, "What does that have to do with today? Why would this ever make me leave you?"

"You know there is nothing I wouldn't do to protect Maura," she said in a barely audible voice, watching as he nodded. "After that night, I threatened to leave him. To live at Da's. But he said he'd kill her first. And then me." She shivered. "I couldn't take the chance. I couldn't risk my baby."

"Oh, Niamh," Cormac murmured.

She rubbed at her sodden face, scrubbing at her chin, where tears dripped to her chest. "He knew Maura was my weakness. And he exploited that. He knew I couldn't refuse him when he threatened her."

"I don't understand," Cormac said, as his fingers stroked over one palm in a soothing touch.

"I'm pregnant with his child, Cormac."

Cormac sat frozen in front of Niamh for long minutes. His gaze unfocused, his expression dumbfounded. He yearned for rage. For indignation. For anything to free him from this frozen paralysis. He jolted when Niamh stroked a hand over his face and stared at her with confusion and torment.

"Say something, please," she whispered.

"When did you know?" he asked. "Was it before ... before our first night at my cabin?" he asked in a hoarse voice, exposing his sense of betrayal. "Before we married?"

"No," she protested, her hand dropping to her lap. "No, Cormac. I just realized this morning, after you left to see Da." She flushed and looked away. "I realized I hadn't had my monthly in too long. I thought it was because of the stress, but I was worried."

"When was your last monthly?" he asked.

"Mid-September," she whispered.

He closed his eyes for a moment, before meeting her devastated gaze again. "Did you see the doctor?" His blue eyes blazed with an unfathomable emotion.

"No, there is no doctor in town during the winter," she said in a barely audible voice. "I visited Nora."

He gripped her arms with a fierce intensity. "What did you do, Niamh?"

Fresh tears leaked from her eyes. "Nothing. Nothing but spoke with her. Allowed her to comfort me." She swallowed a sob. "I thought she could give me a potion, something, but she said she would never do that. That I might die."

At the word *die*, Cormac groaned and hauled her into his embrace, his arms banded around her so tightly that she gasped for breath. "Never, Niamh. Never," he gasped. "You will not die." He rocked her to and fro, as though he were comforting himself as much as her. "And I will not leave you. Ever. You are my wife. And I will honor and cherish you."

"How can you still want me? What will the townsfolk say?" she cried.

He cupped her face and stared deeply into her eyes. "I don't care. All I care is that I love you." He frowned as his words wrought devastation. "Why does my avowal of devotion cause you more distress?" When she shook her head, he whispered, "Do you wish me to leave you?"

"No, Cormac, never. Never. Please, never." Her hands stroked his fingers still caressing her face. "I worry I will prove too great a burden, and you will wish you loved another."

"My love is not fickle, nor is it feeble," he whispered. He stared at her a long moment, frowning as he discerned another unspoken fear. "What is it, beloved?"

Her hands dropped to grip his shoulders, as she fought to speak through her sobs. "I wanted my next baby to have been made in love, not fear and hate. I wanted *our* baby."

He cupped her cheeks, his thumbs swiping her soft skin, while his hands held her in place, so she continued to meet his unwavering gaze. "He or she will be cherished." He kissed her nose. "And we will have our children, Niamh. I promise you."

She curled into his embrace. "How are you such a good man?" she whispered, as she battled falling asleep in his arms.

He refrained from answering, murmuring soft sounds of reassurance, as she slipped into slumber in his embrace. After easing her to the bed, he curled around her, his hands over her belly. Listening to her deep breaths signaling sleep, he pressed his face into the pillow, burying his sobs of distress to again be denied his heart's desire by his brother.

Cormac entered the Bordello, his gaze adjusting to the slightly darkened interior with nooks and crannies in deep shadows. He imagined it aided the Sirens to have a place to tease and to tantalize men before enticing them to their cribs. However, in the morning light, it all looked tawdry, with a hint of desperation. No Siren was about, and he suspected they were sound asleep, after their night's work. A strong hand clapped him on his shoulder, and he turned to meet Ezra's foreboding gaze.

"I hope you didn't come here to cause trouble," Ezra growled. His free hand gripped a billy club, and his glower would send a lesser man running from the Bordello.

Cormac raised an eyebrow, his gaze glinting with amusement. "I'm not Connor. I need to speak with the Madam."

Ezra pointed to a spot near the door. "Wait here."

He half watched Ezra walk down a hallway as Cormac sat in a chair. He closed his eyes, groaning with delight at the comfortable chair. He hoped Ezra had trouble convincing the Madam to see Cormac, as he had no desire to move.

"Townsfolk thought I was a fool to send away for such extravagant furnishings."

"You should charge admittance for permission to sit in them," Cormac murmured, smiling as he met the Madam's amused gaze.

"I do," she said with a wry smile. "It's simply a different sort of charge." She winked at him as he laughed. "Come. I believe we had better speak in private. One never knows who's lurking in a corner."

With great reluctance, Cormac rose from the comfortable chair and followed Madam Nora to her office. She waved him to another chair, watching him intently. After he sat and groaned in delight again, she smiled like a cat that had just eaten the canary.

"Now I know why Seamus visited you with such frequency." He flushed. "Besides your company."

"And my ability to obtain fine whiskey," she said sardonically. "I consider Seamus a great friend. Thus I am loyal to all O'Rourkes and, by extension, to you."

Cormac sobered as he studied the short, but formidable woman. Although barely over five feet tall, she commanded respect. Today, she wore a burgundy satin dress that shimmered in the light, enhancing her subtle beauty. "I know you were loyal to Niamh."

Nora sobered and sat across from him in her comfortable lady's chair. "I will always be loyal to her. Perhaps more loyal to her than to Seamus." She looked at her hands, gripped together on her lap. "She could have had Ezra arrested and charged for the murder of her husband. Of your brother. But she didn't. I will always be indebted to her."

Cormac studied her. "Ezra is more than your employee," he murmured.

She smiled at him and shrugged. "Why did you wish to speak with me?"

"Why didn't you do what Niamh asked you to, if you are indebted to her?"

Nora looked at him with complete innocence and confusion. "I'm afraid I don't understand what you are asking."

"I know Niamh is pregnant. With Connor's child." He spoke in a flat, emotionless voice. "And that she came to you for help yesterday."

Nora let out a sigh, either of frustration or relief. "I believe I did help her. Or are you desirous to be a widower so soon?"

Growling, Cormac canted forward in his seat to the point he almost fell out of it. "You know that's not what I mean. Niamh will not die. She will be with me forever." His blue eyes glowed with sincerity and desperation.

Unable to shield her envy, Nora watched him with awe. "You adore her as a woman dreams of being adored. As she is, with whatever trouble may come her way. Accepting anything and everything, as long as she is with you." When he flushed but remained quiet, Nora whispered, "Don't you?"

He nodded but then murmured, "But it's not adoration. It's love."

Nora relaxed into her chair, staring into the fire. Finally she murmured, "I've seen what potions do to women. Some die. Some can never have another child. And all mourn their loss forever." She met Cormac's gaze. "I would never wish such a fate, whichever it were to be, on Niamh. She deserves happiness and laughter and joy, after the hell of her life with your brother."

"I agree," Cormac whispered. "Thank you for protecting her." He watched as she shrugged, as though her protection of Niamh had always been a foregone conclusion.

Nora was silent for a while longer. "If you do agree with me, you must also come to see that this child is not a penance or a punishment for the love you've felt for each other all throughout her first marriage. This child should never be considered a mistake or a cruel twist of fate." She nodded as she saw a flash of emotion in Cormac's gaze. "Cherish her child as you do her. For she is your woman, your wife, and she needs to know you will support her through every-thing." Nora rose, leaving him alone.

Cormac sat in stunned silence for many moments, considering Nora's wise advice.

~

That morning, Niamh stepped onto the front stoop of the cabin she shared with Cormac, with the intent of walking to her parents' house a short distance away. Cormac had soothed and consoled her the previous day. His first act of devotion was whisking her out of Connor's cabin to his, ensuring she was comfortable and safe. Then, he spoke with her mother about caring for Maura for the rest of the day and evening. Rather than fill the hours with questions and recriminations, he held her in a contented silence, seeming at peace with her mere presence. She had fallen asleep, hopeful and grateful for his devotion.

She paused, tilting her face up to enjoy the sun's rays. Although she was eager to see Maura, as she always was, she relished this moment of peace as she tried to concentrate only on the soothing sensation of the warm rays on her face. She attempted to banish her worries and doubts as readily as the sun heated her but to no avail. Doubts continued to crowd her thoughts, and she feared what her family would say when they learned the truth. She clung to the memory of Cormac holding her, his steadfast love a balm to her doubts.

She heard a snicker, and her eyes snapped open to face Aileen's aunt, Janet Davies. Where Aileen was soft and kind, her aunt was hard-edged and cruel. Niamh had never understood how they were related, but then her two husbands, who were as different as night and day, had been brothers. "Hello, Mrs. Davies," she said, as she descended from her porch step.

Janet, who wore a cranberry wool coat with a fur collar and fur cuffs at the wrists, blocked Niamh's movement and prevented her from easily continuing her walk. "I had thought you'd satisfy him for at least a month," she said in a low, mocking voice, while her eyes gleamed with malicious cruelty.

Taking a deep breath, Niamh stepped to the side to walk around the woman who was becoming the town busybody and gossip. "I have no interest in your gossip or fearmongering."

Janet grabbed her hand and shook her head. "Your husband is at the Bordello, and you don't care? I had thought he was different than Connor, but perhaps the reason was and always has been you, dearest Niamh."

"What?" Niamh asked, unable to hide the shock and disappointment from her voice. "I'm certain you are mistaken. He is at the livery."

Janet cackled with malicious glee. "You're so unwanted, so undesirable, your men have to visit the town brothel to find satisfaction." Her eyes shone with triumph as her words found their mark. "You were such a bother, your mother didn't even want you for years."

"Stop," Niamh gasped, as a few tears coursed down her cheeks. "Leave me be!"

"Niamh?" a soft voice called out.

Niamh looked up to see her mother, Maggie, and Maura walking in her direction. When her mother saw her distress, she handed Maura to Maggie and sent them in the direction of a pile of snow to play in. Mary joined Niamh, poised and polished in a fine ice-blue coat with a lilac scarf, knit by Aileen.

"Hello, Mum."

"Love," Mary murmured. Her voice chilled to the temperature of an arctic breeze. "Mrs. Davies. Always such a tragedy to see you out an' about."

"Tragedy?" Mrs. Davies shrieked. "I have every right to leave the hotel and to talk about the goings-on in town."

Mary nodded, gripping her daughter's hand as she tugged Niamh toward her. Soon Niamh was wrapped in a one-armed embrace by her mother. "Aye, you do, but you should know better than to spread malicious gossip. For one day, 'twill come back to haunt you. Especially since you never seem to have success."

"What are you saying? That my vision is faulty when I saw Niamh's husband go to the Bordello? That he is not as you suspected and a different sort of man than his brother?" Janet said with a note of triumph in her voice, although Mary stared at her with no shock in her gaze. Janet barreled on. "He's as much of a scoundrel as Connor ever was." She looked with scorn in Maura's direction. "As his daughter ever will be."

Niamh stiffened, flushing red. "You leave Maura out of it. She's a sweet girl, not tainted by the viciousness of women like you."

"Aye," Mary said, as she ran a soothing hand down her daughter's back. "An' she's cherished by all who meet her. Just as my Niamh always has been. I know you can imagine my grief at losing my beautiful daughter for so many years and the jubilation to have her back again. And with a granddaughter too. 'Twas as though my heart would burst with the joy of it." She squeezed Niamh.

"You're all delusional," Janet snapped.

Mary laughed. "Perhaps, but then you would say that, as we will have Nora with us for our Christmas celebration. There are those who would believe the owner of the Bordello should not be allowed in good company. However, she's proven to be a good friend to the O'Rourkes." She looked at Janet with guileless cunning before she met Niamh's gaze. "Cormac agreed to visit Nora to invite her. Wasn't that nice of him?"

Janet sputtered and then stormed away.

Niamh leaned against her mother, fighting tears. "Is that true, Mum?" She met her mother's mournful gaze, and her shoulders stooped.

"Come, love," Mary urged. "Play with your daughter, then come to the house for tea and fresh bread I baked this mornin'. I'm sure there's a reason for Cormac to visit Nora." She paused until Niamh met her gaze. "An' 'tisn't Janet's reason."

Niamh hugged Mary, smelling the familiar scents of vanilla and what was all Mary. "Thank you, Mum, for standing up for me. I didn't have the energy today."

"I'll always protect my wee babe," she whispered in her daughter's ear. "I just wish I'd been here all the times you needed me."

Swiping at her cheek, Niamh said, "I thought by the time I was twenty-nine that I wouldn't need you as much as I do."

"Ah, love, if there's one thing we always need, 'tis our mother's love." She kissed Niamh on her cheek and walked with her to join Maggie and Maura playing in the snow.

Cormac stood by the Missouri River, staring at nothing, as his mind raced at everything that had occurred in the previous day. Although he had tried not to allow Niamh's news to change anything, he knew it would. Her focus would turn to the child growing in her womb, not their burgeoning relationship. Fighting a resentment that mortified him, he wished he'd had time with solely Niamh and Maura. A few months for the three of them to discover how to be a family, as the shadow of Connor's ghost faded. Now his ghost would be an ever-present figure in their lives.

Cormac kicked at a rock, watching as it sailed forward and over the bank into the river. Stifling a snort of disgust, he felt like the rock. Kicked and pushed around, until he careened out of control. He took a deep breath, reminding himself that he had never lost his composure with Niamh. He prayed he never would. However, he wished he could go to the Sunrise Saloon and drown his sorrows. He wished he could take a match and burn Connor's house to the ground. If only the effects of Connor's mistreatment could be so easily vanquished.

Ignoring the footsteps that approached, Cormac hoped the townsperson would accept his unfriendliness today and then leave him be. When the person stopped beside him and stared at the river, he swore.

"Not very hospitable toward your brother-in-law," Ardan murmured. "And Happy Christmas Eve."

"Merry Christmas Eve," Cormac muttered. "May you find more joy than I do."

Ardan gaped at him, his blue eyes gleaming with bewilderment. "How can you be miserable? You married Niamh less than a month ago. You've been enjoying nights without your niece. Your step-daughter."

Cormac turned to face his inquisitive brother-in-law. "Ardan, as I'm certain you understand, nothing in life is ever easy."

Ardan tugged at his jacket and wrapped the scarf Deirdre knitted for him tighter around his neck. "Aye," he said. "Deirdre an' I had a rocky relationship in the beginning. As I know you are aware of." He paused. "You an' Niamh have to overcome Connor's memory, but you will, Cormac."

"Tell me *how*, Ardan, when my wife informed me yesterday that she's pregnant with my brother's child," he snapped and then flushed. "Dammit," he rasped, as he closed his eyes, shaking his head. "We were waiting to tell the family tomorrow at Christmas dinner."

Ardan stood frozen beside him at the news. After a few moments, he whispered, "I won't say anything. I won't ruin your surprise."

"It's not a surprise. It's a damn tragedy." He ran a hand through his long hair. "What am I supposed to do, Ardan?"

"What did you do when Niamh told you?" Ardan asked.

"Reassured her. Told her that I'd always care for her and her babe. That the babe would be cherished." He chuckled, but no warmth or humor laced the laugh. "How many times must my brother thwart me?"

"Ah, Cormac," Ardan whispered. He paused, then stared at the chunks of ice floating in the river and the ice coating the riverbank on the distant shore. "I remember one Christmas, a few years after we lost Mum. Colleen was with us, and Niamh was desperate for a moth-er's attention. Affection. She yearned for the softness only another woman could show her. Or a man who loved her."

He faced Cormac now. "But Colleen wasn't such a woman. She had no affection to spare for children who weren't hers from a man who could never love her as he had loved his first wife. I remember seeing wee Niamh, fighting tears, as she tilted up her chin, bravely saying she didn't like to be hugged. She cringed away from most contact from any of us after that, although she always had a soft spot for Da and me."

"Why?" Cormac whispered. "Niamh's always sought out affection from me."

"Exactly," Ardan said. "Because she knows you will never deny her any of her deepest desires. Or mock her needs. You will support her and love her through everything." He looked at Cormac with a heart-felt admiration. "Rather than rail at your fate in front of her, you soothed her and loved her. Loved her unborn babe. That is the measure of the man you are, Cormac."

"Connor continues to take what I most desire," he protested.

"Ah, but has he?" Ardan asked. "Or had you already denied your brother what he most needed?" At Cormac's perplexed stare, Ardan continued. "When Niamh had a problem, who did she turn to? When Niamh was troubled, did she run to Connor? Who did she make the special dinners for?"

Cormac rubbed at his head, as he thought through Ardan's questions.

"Unconsciously, every time she needed something, she turned to you. She knew, even after she'd only been married to Connor a few days, that you were the one she could count on. How do you imagine that made your brother feel?"

Vibrating with tension, Cormac hissed, "Don't pin his abuse on me."

"Never. That is his shame and his alone. However, Niamh knew, deep inside, that you were the man of her heart, even though she was married to your brother. Even now, she knows it. Don't let this tear you apart, Cormac. Continue to love her and her unborn babe."

Cormac covered his eyes a moment. "She doesn't love me, Ardan. I can't tell you the number of times I've told her, and she's never said it back to me."

"What does she call you in Irish?"

Cormac shrugged. "*A shíorghrá.* Although I don't know what it means."

Ardan stared at him in stunned silence for a few moments and then gave him a cryptic smile. "Ask Niamh. That's something a husband should hear from his wife the first time." He squeezed Cormac's shoulder. "Never doubt she cares."

～

N iamh curled onto her side, stiffening when Cormac attempted to wrap an arm around her waist. When he kissed the back of her neck, she shivered, but not from any burgeoning passion. "Stop it," she hissed. "Don't touch me!" She tossed his hand away and scooted as far as she could to her edge of the bed until she nearly toppled out of it.

"Niamh," Cormac rasped, his voice filled with hurt and shock. "What did I do? What's happened?" He reached forward and stilled her frenetic movements, preventing her from falling out of the bed. When she turned onto her side to face him, he held up his hands. "I promise I won't touch you." He swallowed at the devastation in her gaze. "But tell me what happened. Please."

"You should know," she snapped.

Shaking his head, dumbfounded, he grunted when she hit him on his chest. "Niamh, talk with me. This never resolves anything."

"You went to the Bordello!" she screeched, sitting up, so she was on her knees and looming over him. Her cheeks were flushed red, and her eyes were filled with rage and betrayal. "How could you do that to me after what Connor did?"

"Oh, love," Cormac murmured, raising a hand to caress her face. But, when he saw her flinch away from any contact with him, he dropped his hand to his side. "Listen, please." He frowned. "I can only imagine what the gossips of this town said, but they're all wrong."

"Did you go there?" she demanded, her hands fisted together on her thighs.

He nodded, acceding that point. "Fine, they're not wrong about that. I did go there. This morning. To speak with the Madam." He saw her eyes flare with an unidentifiable emotion. Shame? Guilt? Hope? He couldn't determine as it was so fleeting. "No Siren was around, as they are all abed at that hour." He smiled with tenderness as she flushed at that news. "I have no need of anyone's touch, Niamh. Nor do I desire anyone but you. Please believe me."

She let out a deep breath, her righteous indignation and rage seeming to seep out of her with her breath. Now she sat, deflated and defeated, in front of him. "Why did you go there?" she asked in a low voice.

"We are to have a baby," he said, smiling softly as her gaze flew to his, filled with wonder and surprise at his words. "I wanted to speak with Nora. To confront her about what she had and had not done." His voice dropped to a barely audible level. "To thank her for protecting you and for not giving you a potion."

"I would have thought you'd challenge her for not giving me one." She took a deep breath. "I could still try to procure one if you want."

"No!" He reached forward, gripping one of her hands and squeezing it tight. "No, Niamh, please don't do that to me."

She stared at him in confusion, her gaze filled with wonderment at his panic. "I don't understand."

He moved toward her slowly, his alert gaze gauging her reaction and the tension easing as she did not stiffen up at his approach. Soon he knelt in front of her, their knees touching, his hands on her shoulders. Leaning forward, his forehead touched hers. He breathed, "Nothing can ever happen to you, Niamh. You are my wife. My love. You are precious, Niamh, and I can bear anything but for you to be harmed. Or Maura. Or the babe we are to have."

"*We?*" she whispered, her gaze filled with trepidation and hope. "Are you sure?"

He nodded, opening his arms to her. When she crawled into his embrace and didn't protest his touch, he let out a stuttering sigh of relief. "Please don't shut me out again. Talk with me. Believe in me, not the horrible gossips of this town."

She tightened her hold of him before whispering her promise. "I will. Always."

CHAPTER 15

The sound of his boots scrunching on the snow echoed over the barren land, and he pulled his coat tighter around him. He still didn't have a scarf or hat and hoped one of the O'Rourke women had taken pity on him and had knitted him a replacement for his lost and destroyed items for Christmas presents. He smiled ironically, noting he was thinking about inconsequential matters rather than focusing on his latest heartache. Or his ongoing battle with his dead brother. He stopped, staring at the nondescript marker, as the memory of that long-ago night when everything changed came flooding back.

"I'm sorry he hurt you," Cormac whispered. "I should have known. I should have paid attention." He stared at her with a mixture of shame and sadness.

"There was nothing you could do," Niamh whispered, as she forced herself to continue to meet his gaze.

"Oh, you are wrong, lo—" He closed his eyes as he broke off speaking the endearment. After a long moment, he opened his eyes, fearful of meeting her gaze, which he knew would be filled with embarrassed compassion as she beheld the man she'd only ever considered brother. When he looked deeply into her gaze and instead saw wonder and disbelief, his heart leapt. "Niamh?"

"I never ..." She shrugged.

He took a slow step toward her, cupping her face. "I would have held you, for as long as you needed to cry. And then I would have found ice, to soothe your aches. And then I would have kissed every one of the places he had dared to hurt you." His blue eyes shone with sincerity and devotion. "I would prove to you that you are cherished."

"Cormac," she breathed. "I ... I don't deserve such—"

He broke off what more she would have said with a soft kiss. When she groaned and gripped his shoulders, arching into him to return his kiss, he hauled her against him, wrapping his strong arms around her. Deepening the kiss, he became deaf and dumb to everything but the wonder of holding the woman of his dreams in his arms. Of kissing her. And having her desire his attentions.

Belatedly, the sound of the door slamming shut registered, and he broke the kiss. Looking over his shoulder, he saw his brother, standing with fists clenched and hatred in his gaze.

"How dare you?" Connor rasped, as he took a threatening step in their direction.

Cormac moved to stand in front of Niamh, protecting her. "I dare because you are a horrible husband, and she deserves to know what it is to be revered." He raised his arm, warding off his brother's blow. Although strong, Connor was no match for Cormac.

"You defiler. You betrayer of a sacred trust!" Connor bellowed. "I thought you were my brother, and all this time you've been lusting after what was never yours. You're despicable, and I'm ashamed to have ever called you brother."

"You're ashamed to call me brother?" Cormac demanded in a low, menacing voice. "Imagine how I feel? A lazy, worthless, layabout schemer whose only claim to fame is his ability to nearly drink himself to death each night."

"Bastard!" Connor bellowed. "I protected you! I kept you from starving when everyone died. You owe me."

Cormac shook his head. "I owe you nothing. You stole my heart's desire and then failed to cherish her. How could you, Connor?"

The brothers stood, glaring at each other, as though attempting to find a way to land a lethal blow.

"Connor," Niamh whispered.

"And you!" Connor screamed at Niamh, as he peered over Cormac's shoulder. "You're a heartless hussy who never brought me a moment's worth of joy. You were born an inadequate daughter, unwanted and unloved by her mother, who was relieved to fake her death rather than to suffer raising you. And you will die an unwanted, repulsive wife."

"You know we're miserable," Niamh whispered.

"Because you are a faithless shrew! How could you do this to me? To our daughter?" He pushed at Cormac, but Cormac met him, and they scrappled until finally Cormac shoved him, and Connor tumbled backward into the door.

"Mark my words," Connor gasped, as he raised his hand and pointed at the two of them, "you will die as disappointments, with no mourners and no one crying over your graves."

"Connor," Niamh whispered again.

"I never loved you, you faithless harpy." Connor stormed from the room, the door slamming shut so hard it rattled the china in the cabinets.

Niamh gasped, falling to her knees, as Cormac stood in stunned silence, unable to offer the comfort they both so desperately needed.

He shivered with cold, returning to the present. "What a fool I am," he muttered to himself, as he studied Connor's grave. "You'd think I'd be filled with a sense of accomplishment. A sense that I'd finally outmatched you." He ran a hand through his hair, sprinkled with a dusting of light snow.

"But you always win, don't you?" He glared at his brother's marker. "You always have the last word." He bowed his head before dropping to his knees. "Damn you, brother," he rasped, as he fought a sob. His shoulders shook as he lost his battle with his deep emotions. "Damn you for always denying me what I most want in this world."

He swiped at his cheeks and reached forward, cleaning off the little bit of snow that clung to Connor's marker. "This is my first Christmas without you. The first Christmas I haven't had my big brother by my side. I know now what you were to Niamh, and, even though you never worked with me here in Fort Benton, you were a good brother to me after we lost our family." He bent forward as he continued to sob. "How could the boy who protected me from the Chichesters, the boy who taught me to never hit my sister, the boy who worked so diligently on our parents' farm"—he paused, gasping a few times between his tears—"how could you have turned into the man who would beat his wife, who threatened his daughter, and who refused to work to help his family?"

He dug his hands into the snow at his side and shook his head. "I mourn the boy you were, Connor. I will always mourn him, for he was a kind, good older brother." With a deep breath, he looked at the marker. "But I will only ever exult that you died. For the boy I knew had already died, replaced by a selfish monster."

Pushing himself to his feet, Cormac brushed away the tears at his cheeks and spoke in a self-assured, determined voice. "I will love Niamh forever. I will cherish Maura. And I will adore and love Niamh's babe. For that babe will only ever know she is treasured." He took one last deep breath, whispered, "Merry Christmas," and turned on his heel to return to the cabin to be there when Niamh awoke.

~

Niamh set Maura down in the O'Rourke kitchen, smiling, as her daughter raced from person to person for a kiss and a hug. She tugged on her uncles until one of them walked with her into the living room, where a small mound of presents sat in one corner.

"No openin' presents until we're all together," Mary called out.

"An' no cheatin'!" Seamus hollered, with a wink to his children who lingered in the kitchen.

Niamh took a deep breath, closing her eyes at the scents wafting through the air. Mulled cider vied with fresh-baked bread and the scent of roasting venison. She breathed deeply again before murmuring, "Reminds me of Christmases when I was a lass."

Mary wrapped an arm around her waist and squeezed her. "Aye, 'twas what I was hoping for, although we have more food now than we ever did then."

"But we never had venison," Kevin said with a chuckle, as he held Aileen in his arms.

"No," Niamh said, as she looked at her cheerful family, gathered here. She fought tears as she saw them dressed in their Sunday best but with touches of red and green to mark the holiday spirit. "'Tis hard to believe we are together, with three of us happily married this year."

"Ah, but too many of the lads are missin'," Seamus said. "I pray they are enjoyin' their time in Saint Louis and are not into any mischief."

Ardan laughed, as he watched Deirdre bustle around the kitchen, helping his mother. "You know the twins will be raisin' havoc, while Declan attempts to keep them in line." He sighed and shook his head. "I don't envy him."

"I wonder if one, or more, of them will return home with a bride," Deirdre said. She stilled in her movements around the kitchen, as conversations ground to a halt at her comment. "What?" she asked.

Mary shook her head. "'Tis I who's bein' foolish. I've always hoped to be present at every marriage. I asked each lad, before he left, that, if he did find a fine woman, to bring her home to marry here. We'll have to see if they will comply."

Seamus kissed Mary's head. "They will. For none of us ever wants to disappoint you, *a ghrá*."

Mary flushed at the murmurs of agreement.

Niamh moved to stand in Cormac's sheltering embrace, watching her family interact. The younger boys still had the youthful anticipation of Christmas mornings, although Bryan and Henri were trying to emulate their older siblings. However, they were unable to hide their eagerness to open presents and then to eat the bountiful feast.

"Thank you," Cormac whispered in her ear.

She turned her head, her gaze showing her bewilderment.

"Thank you for making me a full-fledged member of this madness. I'd hate to always be on the outside, wishing I were here. With you."

"Oh, Cormac," she breathed, kissing him softly. She rested her head on his chest, joy filling her to be in her husband's arms, as she fought panic at all that would be revealed today to her family.

~

After presents were opened, the fire stoked, and cups of mulled cider had been drunk, the family milled in the living room before eating supper. Dunmore and Nora were to arrive soon for the elaborate meal. Cormac gripped Niamh's hand as they stood to one side, watching everyone laugh, tell stories, or play games. He whispered in her ear, "Is now the time?"

She stiffened and then nodded. "I hate to ruin the good mood," she whispered. "Everyone is so happy." She had turned into his arms, so it looked as though the newlyweds were canoodling.

"This is good news, Niamh." He kissed her neck and smiled encouragingly at her. He cleared his throat, as Niamh pressed more firmly against him and began to softly shake. "If I could make an announcement?"

"No," Niamh protested. She shook her head at Cormac, as he sighed with disappointment behind her. "I have an announcement to make." She flushed and cleared her throat, as her boisterous family eventually calmed. "I ... I'm expecting a baby."

"Oh, Niamh!" Mary exclaimed rushing toward her and pulling her into her arms. "What wondrous news." She clasped her close, rocking her in her arms. "Another babe to love and to cherish."

Seamus approached, his joy less exuberant than his wife's. "Congratulations, Niamh." He shared a long look with Cormac and then nodded. "I hope you are feeling well."

"More tired than I like to admit," she said. She bravely accepted all her siblings' words of felicitation, until she was once again with her parents, Ardan, Deirdre, Kevin, Aileen, and Maggie. Cormac had never left her side.

"What aren't you telling us, Niamh?" Kevin asked, as he saw the subtle tension his sister attempted to conceal and Cormac's forced joviality.

Niamh relaxed as Cormac wrapped an arm around her waist, tugging her back into him. "The babe is Connor's," she whispered.

At the gasps from her mother, sister, and sisters-in-law, Niamh ducked her head.

"When did you discover you were with child?" Mary asked, her soft touch stroking her daughter's head.

"A few days ago. I realized …" She flushed, unwilling to discuss such a personal matter with her brothers or father. "And then I visited Nora."

Seamus stiffened. "Nora," he said in a low, threatening voice. "What did she recommend?"

"That I tell my husband and learn to love this babe," Niamh said, with a defiant tilt of her head.

"Seamus," Mary admonished her husband, turning to stroke a hand down his arms. "You're not helping anything." When Seamus relaxed under her touch, Mary focused on her daughter and Cormac. "Wise words, and I would have expected nothing less from her, after spending so much time with her, when she lived with us." Mary's gaze searched Cormac's guarded gaze and frowned. "How are you, Cormac?"

"Fine," he murmured, his hold on his wife tightening incrementally.

Seamus muttered a curse at the word but quieted as Mary nudged him in his side with her elbow.

Cormac stared at his father-in-law, his expression severe and foreboding. "Niamh and I will be parents again come summer. For Maura is mine now, and I couldn't love her more than I already do. As I will love this baby."

"Cormac," Niamh whispered, as she turned into his arms, wrapping her hands around his waist.

"Our child will know love," he avowed. He stared at those he considered family, as though daring them to contradict him.

"Of course she will," Deirdre whispered, her eyes filled with tears as she watched him soothe and cuddle Niamh. "You are a good man, Cormac."

He kissed Niamh's forehead and then her head. "No, I love my wife. I'll love her through everything. Anything."

Seamus beamed at him and gripped his arm. He raised his voice, garnering the attention of the younger lads, who had moved away to play in a corner of the room. "Such joyous news calls for a celebration. My wee Niamh will bless us with a babe come summer, an' we'll have more reasons to give thanks."

Niamh kissed Cormac's jaw, before easing from his hold and facing her father. "Da," she whispered. "I feared you'd be angry with me."

Seamus pulled her into his embrace. "Never, my Niamh," he whispered in her ear. "You survived. And now your eyes will be filled with happiness as you await your babe with your husband beside you."

She kissed his cheek and then moved to hug her mother again, while Seamus found a small barrel of whiskey in the root cellar. Cormac stood beside her, clasping her hand. Soon they all had a glass, and they raised it high.

"To family. To perseverance. To love." Seamus raised his glass higher. "*Sláinte.*"

"*Sláinte!*"

After the toast by Seamus, Niamh stood alone to the side of the gathering, watching as Cormac spoke with her brothers and father. She shook her head with bemusement at the amount of back-slapping and chest puffing. "Male pride," she murmured, as she stared at her husband with covetous eyes. She never failed to marvel that such an incredible man had fallen in love with her.

"Niamh," Deirdre murmured, pulling her close. "I'm so happy for you, although I don't know what I will do next summer season without your help in the café kitchen." Her self-deprecating smile faded as she saw Niamh battling tears. "Are you well?"

"Oh, I am. I'm crying more due to the babe." She leaned forward to hug Deirdre and then stepped back. "I don't know what I would have done last summer without your friendship. Thank you." She swiped at her cheeks, smudging her tears. With a murmur of appreciation, she accepted a handkerchief from Deirdre.

Deirdre chuckled. "I fear you have it all backward. I would have been lost without you and your friendship, Niamh." She squeezed Niamh's hand. After a moment's pause, Deirdre subtly turned so her back was to the room and so her face wasn't visible to other O'Rourkes. "Cormac treats you well, Niamh?"

At Niamh's shocked expression, Deirdre paled. "What are you asking, Deirdre?"

"Please tell me that he's nothing like his brother," she whispered.

Niamh shook her head, her hands over her belly, as though protecting her babe. "No, he's the opposite. Kind. Loving. Wonderful." She frowned with bewilderment as she stared at Deirdre. "Why would you doubt?"

Deirdre let out a breath and flushed. "Last summer, I knew you'd been … mistreated." She took another deep breath. "Beaten. But you wanted me to say nothing to your family. I was estranged from Ardan, and I'd clung to enough of my own secrets that I didn't feel I could force you to give up yours." She bit her lip and then whispered, "When I pushed you a little one day, you said both their names. Connor and Cormac. I feared they'd both harmed you."

Niamh paled and swayed, as though she were to fall. Deirdre gripped her arm, steadying her. "No, Dee, never Cormac. It's when he discovered the truth. When he saw me battered." Her hazel eyes shone with shame. "I forgot to lock the door one day, and he waltzed in to see me …" Her hand flitted around, as though that were explanation enough.

"Oh, Niamh," Deirdre breathed, as she pulled her close. "I've been so worried. Terrified. And uncertain what I should say. Everyone in the family has been delighted at your relationship, and I've lived with such fear all this time."

"There's no need. He's nothing like his brother. He'd never hurt me."

Deirdre released her and swiped at her cheeks. "Good." She beamed at her friend. "Be happy, Niamh. That is my wish for you."

Niamh returned her sister-in-law and good friend's smile. "I am. And I know I will continue to be. Thank you, Deirdre, for being loyal to me." Her eyes shone with incredulity. "I never thought I deserved that in the past."

"You do. That and so much more."

Cormac watched as Niamh readied for bed. They had left a sleeping Maura in the care of her parents and Maggie, so Cormac and his bride could enjoy their first Christmas night together at his cabin. She had slipped into a thick flannel nightgown that should not have stirred his ardor, but he realized that, anytime Niamh was in the room with him, he would desire her. No matter what she wore. She sat on their bed, her fingers working to braid her long auburn hair, and she held the ribbon between her teeth. He approached her, his gaze solemn as he slipped the ribbon free. "Let me," he murmured as he tied the ribbon to the base of her braid. After kissing her hair, he set the long plait against her chest.

Rather than kiss her, he knelt in front of her. "Niamh," he breathed, as he bowed his head. "I must ask your forgiveness."

Her hands played in his loose hair before she raked them through his beard. "*Forgiveness*. What have you done, Cormac?"

"I have carried an anger, a resentment inside me these past few days. I'm so sorry." His blue eyes glinted with remorse as he stared deeply into her gaze. "You are so beautiful, my bride. My Niamh." He gazed at her, as though she were lit by the sun rather than the faint light of a candle.

"I've always felt beautiful to you," she whispered.

After a long pause, he closed his eyes before murmuring, "I wish your baby were mine, Niamh." A tear trickled down his cheek. "I wish —" When her fingers covered his mouth, his eyes flew open so he could meet her gaze.

"*Shh.*" She stared at him with unutterable tenderness, her beautiful eyes gleaming with unshed tears. "How can you not understand I wish it were too?"

He kissed her fingers and gazed deeply into her eyes. "I realized today, as I stood watching you with your family. With Maura. I realized I will love every child we share." His eyes gleamed with love. "I will love this child as if it were mine, made from an insurmountable love. For that is how I love you, Niamh."

Her eyes filled, and she nodded.

"No matter how many children we have, I will never love Maura and this babe less. I promise you."

"Oh, Cormac," she gasped, as she reached for him, burying her face in his neck. "This is my most precious Christmas gift."

He waited, but she remained quiet in his arms. Finally he whispered, "Why can't you tell me?" When she stiffened in his arms, he eased her away. "Why must I wait, wondering if you truly feel the same?" His eyes glowed with hurt and hope.

She opened and closed her mouth a few times. Finally she whispered, "*A shíorghrá*, you know how I feel." Paling as he shook his head, she clung to his shoulders and kissed him with a quiet desperation.

"What does that mean?" he rasped, when he broke their kiss.

"*My eternal love*," she breathed. When she saw the shock and delight in his expression, she smiled and repeated it in a louder, more confident voice. "For you are my eternal love, Cormac. You always have been."

"But you married Connor first."

She flushed in embarrassment. "Yes, I've thought a lot about when I first met you and Connor. I'm ashamed to admit I didn't believe I deserved the love of a man like you, Cormac. I thought you deserved someone better. Smarter, prettier." She paused as she saw the flash of anger in his gaze. "Someone who didn't kill her mother and baby sister by giving them typhus."

"Niamh," he whispered, pulling her off the bed and into his lap on the floor. "You were never to blame, and I hate how you suffered because of that belief."

She wrapped her arms and legs around him, clinging to him like a vine. "I thought I deserved no better than Connor. That the little attention I received from him was all I deserved and all the more precious because it was fleeting and rare." She rested her head on Cormac's shoulder. "I know now what a fool I was. I deserve a man who isn't afraid to hold my hand as we walk through town. Who will kiss me, even though Da or my brothers might see. A man who believes I'm beautiful and smart." She inched back and stared deeply into her husband's gaze. "I deserve you, Cormac."

"Yes, you do, my beloved. Thank God you realize that," he whispered, as he peppered soft kisses all over her face and down her neck as she arched back. "For I deserve you. A wife unabashedly passionate. Loving and kind and considerate. Affectionate," he whispered into her ear, as she shivered with delight. "Loyal, giving, and a wonderful mother." He paused in kissing his way down to her shoulder to stare into her eyes with a look of absolute wonder. "How can such a beautiful woman be my wife?"

She beamed at him. "I feel the same about you, husband."

He laughed, helping her up and onto the bed. "Good, we can marvel at our good fortune together." He eased her nightgown up. "Let me love you, Niamh, on our first Christmas together. Let me show you how I love you."

"Yes," she whispered, "as I'll show you."

~

They lay cuddled under the covers, as the fire crackled in the stove. Niamh rested her head on his shoulder and traced patterns on her husband's chest. "What are you thinking about, love?"

He shivered and kissed the top of her head. "I'll never tire of hearing you call me your love." His eyes gleamed with joy as he beheld her, well-loved and happy in his embrace. "I was dreaming about our future." He paused and then said, "When the spring comes, your da and brothers have agreed to help me. We are going to use the wood from your old home to expand our home here." He looked around the small room he cherished. "This will become a bedroom or our kitchen."

"Oh, Cormac," she breathed, "but that will be so much work."

"You're worth it, beloved. As is our family." He sighed as she curled up even closer against him. "I envision nights like this, with our children asleep in bed, as we share our hopes and fears with each other." He paused. "Or where we rest in silence, knowing there is nothing we need to say."

She propped her head on her hands, smiling at him. "I've always cherished the silence as much as the conversation with you. In a family as large as mine, silence is precious."

After kissing her nose, he murmured, "I saw you speaking with Deirdre tonight. You seemed surprised by what she said."

Niamh sighed. "She worried you were like Connor." When Cormac stiffened underneath her, she ran a soothing hand over his chest. "Last summer, in August, I didn't go to work for a few days at the café. I told her that Maura had been ill." She flushed. "Somehow she figured out what I had suffered, but I stammered out both your names." Her hazel eyes were filled with guilt. "Deirdre had no way of knowing if one or both of you were responsible for causing me harm."

"Oh, Niamh," Cormac whispered, as he pulled her close.

"I swear I never meant to give rise to any doubt as to your honor."

"No, love, it doesn't matter. She understands now."

Niamh sighed, resting in her husband's arms. After a long moment, she whispered, "Promise me."

"Anything," he breathed.

"Promise me this is no dream."

He cupped her face, staring deeply into her luminescent hazel eyes. "This is better than any dream. For every day I know I will awaken with heaven in my arms. And I could never want for more than that."

"Oh, Cormac," she whispered as she kissed him. "Promise me this will never change. That we will never change."

He smiled. "We *will* change, my beloved. But my love for you will be forever constant."

SNEAK PEEK AT PIONEER LONGING!

We join in on a scene where Phoebe and Eamon chat for the first time in the novel...

Missouri River, May 1866

When Phoebe Mortimer heard the voices of the O'Rourke brothers approaching, she admitted to herself that they were the reason why she tried to always appear put together. Since she had first seen them on the steamboat, she had felt an affinity with them. Upon meeting the brothers, her attraction to the older brother, Eamon had grown. However, Eamon seemed interested in friendship, and she feared he only saw her as another sibling, not as a woman he would choose to court and wed.

She shook her head in consternation as she knew she should not be concerning herself with thoughts of marriage. She should be worried about her missing uncle. Admonishing herself for her selfish thoughts, she turned with an impersonal smile to greet the brothers as they stepped into the shaded area. "Hello," she breathed.

"Miss Mortimer," Finn said with a smile.

Winnifred snorted from the ground. "You could be speaking to the three of us, not Phoebe."

"Aye, I could, but seein' as you're sitting on the ground on an anthill, an' you're other sister is engaged in a book, I thought I'd address my greeting to the woman who seemed sensible and friendly." Finn's blue eyes flashed with distaste as he stared at Winnifred. When she jumped up and patted at her skirts, belatedly realizing they were covered in red ants, he chuckled.

Eamon bit back a laugh as he slapped a hand on his younger brother's shoulder. "Hello, Miss Phoebe," he said in his low baritone, his cobalt blue eyes focusing on her for a moment. "'Tis lovely to see you, and your sisters. We hope you don't mind us invading your sanctuary, but we found ourselves in need of company."

At Winnifred's snort of disbelief, Phoebe approached them and motioned the brothers to join her sisters. She glared at her youngest sister until she bit her lip and was quiet. "We are uncertain how long we are to wait."

Eamon looked at the boat and shrugged. "I fear it could be a day or two until they discern what's to be done."

"Must we sleep off the boat?"

Eamon shrugged. "I doubt they'd ask that of you, Miss Phoebe. Although I imagine we'll have to be careful as we are more vulnerable to an Indian attack while tied up on the side of the river at night."

"Attack?" Phoebe gasped, paling.

"Eamon," Finn muttered, hitting him in his arm.

At Winnifred's proclamation that she could shoot better than any man present, Finn wandered off to bicker with her, leaving Phoebe and Eamon alone. "You are well, Miss?" he asked. At her subtle nod, he whispered, "Do you need anything?"

She shrugged. "I need to be on my way to Fort Benton. I need to determine what happened to my uncle. We all do."

Eamon stared at her in confusion. "That's why you're travelin' up river?" At her shrug, he smiled. "I assumed you were mail order brides and already promised to men upstream."

She flushed and gasped and shook her head frantically. "Oh, no.

No, no, no." Biting her lip to cease repeating the same word like a senseless ninny, she blushed as bright as the previous night's sunset. "I don't know how you could have come to that erroneous conclusion."

Eamon's lips quirked up into a smile, and he ran a hand through his inky black hair, now worn longer than usual as he mimicked his older brother, Declan. "My second eldest brother, Kevin, met a woman on a steamboat last year. She was promised to my brother Declan, although neither knew it."

Phoebe gasped, her green eyes lit with interest. "What happened? Did he break your brother's heart?" Her gaze veered to her sisters and then back to Eamon, and she reddened at his astute gaze.

"No, Declan didn't know Aileen as Kev did. Declan didn't care for her as Kev did. In the end, Kevin married her, after rescuing her from the Bordello." When she gasped again, he winked at her. "So, you can see why I'd be cautious about meeting a woman on the steamboat."

Preening a little, Phoebe, tilted her head back, hoping it showed off the fine length of her neck or the delicate curve of her earlobe.

"Besides, you remind me of my youngest sister, Maggie. 'Tis always nice to have good company on a long journey."

Fighting the urge to collapse at his feet in dismay in a pool of petticoats and lace edged skirts, she looked away from him on the pretense of studying the men working on the steamboat. After blinking rapidly to clear her eyes of unwanted, and, she feared, unwarranted tears, she motioned in the direction of the men laboring to move the steamboat over the sandbar. "It seems they need strong men to aid the captain's plan. Why don't you and your brother help?" she asked, clearing her throat to rid it of any huskiness from an excess of emotion.

Eamon shrugged, his eyes lit with an inner warmth as he looked at her. "We offered, but after we helped unload the supplies, he informed us we'd done enough. Doesn't want to hurt his reputation by becoming known that he has the men rentin' private cabins doing such menial labor." He shrugged and winked at her. "And then we realized he doesn't have a clue what he's doin', so we're hidin' away so he doesn't get it into his head to put us to work again."

Phoebe flushed at his wink and her gaze flit over him, taking in his broad shoulders and the muscles that rippled under his shirt with each movement. "I'd think you were used to menial labor." She blushed a brighter hue of red at her comment. Stammering, she blurted out, "I beg your pardon. I meant no offense."

"None, taken Miss. Aye, we're used to workin' hard. Our Da would have it no other way." His gaze was distant for a moment before he smiled at her in a reassuring manner. "We might be successful now, but Finn and I work hard. As do all the O'Rourkes. None are lazy."

Phoebe stiffened as though he had criticized her family. "Mortimers are hard workers, too, Mr. O'Rourke."

"Aye, of that I have no doubt," he murmured with a soft chuckle. "I can imagine how much hard labor goes into reading a novel, over and over again."

Flushing, Phoebe fisted her hands at her side as she took a step toward him, her shoulders back as though challenging him. "Leave Lorena out of this," she whispered. "She's done nothing to earn such criticism from you."

His cheeks turned red and he ducked his head. "I beg your pardon," he whispered. "I fear we are acting like Finn and your sister." He glanced in their direction, snorting with disbelief to see Winnifred standing on tiptoe as she poked Finn in his shoulder as she expounded on her point. Eamon focused on Phoebe, his stance relaxing and his blue eyes filled with regret. "I have no desire to quarrel with you, Miss Phoebe," he murmured. "I...Too often in our past we've been deemed less worthy because we are immigrants and willing to do whatever work we must to survive."

Phoebe took a deep breath and stared deeply into his gaze. "I don't understand what that life is like," she said in a soft voice. "But I do understand fighting against prejudice." She paused, and appeared as though debating whether to say more. "I forgive you, Mr. O'Rourke."

"Eamon," he whispered. "There are too many Mr. O'Rourkes, but I'm the only Eamon. Thank you, Bee." He smiled as she gasped at the use of a nickname. "Is it wrong for me to think of you as Bee?"

She swallowed. Finally, she breathed, "I've only ever been Phoebe."

"You're much more than only Phoebe." He stilled as the steamboat whistle sounded. "Come, let me help you back to the boat. I fear they've given up for the day, and we'll have to see what tomorrow brings."

Phoebe fought a girlish blush as she slipped her hand through his offered arm, reminding herself he was being a gentleman. And he only saw her as a friend. Anything to lessen her growing attraction to this unattainable man.

Order Pioneer Longing Now! Available to read August 4, 2020!

NEVER MISS A RAMONA FLIGHTNER UPDATE!

Thank you for reading *Pioneer Yearning*! I hope you enjoyed it as much as I enjoyed writing it.

I love hearing from you, so please feel free to write me and let me know what you think!

You can reach me at: ramona@ramonaflightner.com

Join My Newsletter For Updates, and Sneak Peeks about the series you love!

Want new release alerts, access to bonus materials and exclusive give-aways, and all my announcements first? Subscribe to my weekly newsletter!

Want to be notified about freebies and sales? Try Bookbub!

Want to stay up to date on new releases, my life in beautiful Montana, and research trip adventures? Find Me On Facebook! Or Find Me On Instagram!

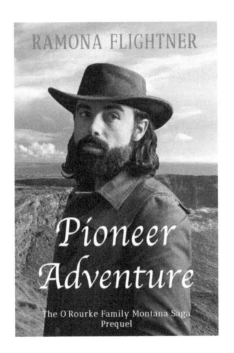

Bear Grass Springs Series

Never fear, I am busy at work on the next book in the series! If you want to make sure you never miss a release, a special, a cover reveal, or a short story just for my fans, sign up for my newsletter!

Immerse yourself in 1880's Montana as the MacKinnon siblings and their extended family find love!

Montana Untamed (BGS, Book 1)- Cailean and Annabelle

Montana Grit (BGS, Book 2)- Alistair and Leticia

Montana Maverick (BGS, Book 3) Ewan and Jessamine

Montana Renegade(BGS, Book 4) Warren and Helen

Jubilant Montana Christmas (BGS, Book 5) Leena and Karl

Montana Wrangler (BGS, Book 6) Sorcha and Frederick

Unbridled Montana Passion (BGS, Book 7) Fidelia and Bears

Montana Vagabond (BGS, Book 8) Ben and Jane

Exultant Montana Christmas (BGS, Book 9) Ewan and Jessamine

Lassoing a Montana Heart (BGS, Book 10) Slims and Davina—Coming July 2020!

Healing Montana Love (BGS, Book 11) Coming in 2020!

The Banished Saga

Follow the McLeod, Sullivan and Russell families as they find love, their loyalties are tested, and they overcome the challenges of their time. A sweeping saga set between Boston and Montana in early 1900's America. Finally, the Saga is complete!

The Banished Saga: (In Order)

Love's First Flames (Prequel)

Banished Love

Reclaimed Love

Undaunted Love (Part One)

ABOUT RAMONA

Ramona is a historical romance author who loves to immerse herself in research as much as she loves writing. A native of Montana, every day she marvels that she gets to live in such a beautiful place. When she's not writing, her favorite pastimes are fly fishing the cool clear streams of a Montana river, hiking in the mountains, and spending time with family and friends.

Ramona's heroines are strong, resilient women, the type of women you'd love to have as your best friend. Her heroes are loyal and honorable, men you'd love to meet or bring home to introduce to your family for Sunday dinner. She hopes her stories bring the past alive and allow you to forget the outside world for a while.

BB bookbub.com/authors/ramona-flightner

pinterest.com/Ramonaauthor

facebook.com/authorramonaflightner

instagram.com/rflightner

Made in the USA
Las Vegas, NV
09 March 2021